Chantelle Shaw lives on the Kent coast and thinks up her stories while walking on the beach. She has been married for over thirty years and has six children. Her love affair with reading and writing Mills & Boon stories began as a teenager, and her first book was published in 2006. She likes strong-willed, slightly unusual characters. Chantelle also loves gardening, walking and wine!

Discover more at millsandboon.co.uk

HIRED FOR ROMANO'S PLEASURE

CHANTELLE SHAW

MILLS & BOON

First Published in Great Britain 2018
by Mills & Boon, an imprint of HarperCollins*Publishers*
1 London Bridge Street, London, SE1 9GF

© 2018 Chantelle Shaw

ISBN: 978-0-263-93416-8

MIX
Paper from
responsible sources
FSC™ C007454

Printed and bound in Spain
by CPI, Barcelona

CHAPTER ONE

'I DON'T UNDERSTAND why you invited your ex-wife's daughter to your birthday celebrations.'

Torre Romano could not hide his irritation as he turned away from the window at Villa Romano and looked across the study at his father. Moments ago he had been enjoying the stunning view of the Amalfi coastline—although he was of the opinion that the views from his own house in Ravello, higher up the cliffs, were better. But the bombshell his father had just dropped had re-awoken the complicated emotions that Orla Brogan evoked in him. *Still.*

'I invited my stepson,' Giuseppe said mildly. 'Why wouldn't I also invite my stepdaughter?'

'It's different with Jules. He came to live here with his mother when he was a young boy and you are the only father he has ever known.' Torre looked away from Giuseppe's astute gaze. 'I barely remember Orla,' he said, frustrated that it was not true. 'The only time I met her was eight years ago when you married her mother. The marriage did not last for more than a handful of years,' he reminded Giuseppe drily. 'I know that Orla used to visit Kimberly here, but I must have been away on those occasions and I never saw her again.'

An unbidden memory flashed into Torre's mind of Orla lying beneath him, her milky-pale skin a stark contrast to his dark tan and her hair spread like amber silk across the pillows. Unbelievably he felt his body stir. *Dio!* How could she still affect him all these years after he had spent just one night with her? he wondered grimly.

But the truth was that Orla was the only woman who had ever made him lose control. Eight years ago he'd taken one look at her and the promise he'd made to himself—that he would never be led by his libido, like his father—had been swept away on a riptide of lust. It had been shameful proof that he had inherited Giuseppe's weakness for pretty women and sex.

Torre pulled his mind back to the present when he realised that his father was speaking again. 'Orla has not been back here in the four years since her mother left me and hired a top divorce lawyer,' Giuseppe said ruefully. 'But I remain fond of her and I am pleased that both my stepchildren are coming to Amalfi to help me celebrate my seventieth birthday. I wonder if Jules will use the occasion to make an announcement?'

'An announcement about what?' Torre's brows rose.

'That he plans to marry Orla. Don't look so surprised. I'm sure I mentioned that Jules had met up with her when he moved to London a few months ago to work at the English branch of ARC. Recently he has hinted that he has stronger feelings for her than simply friendship. Perhaps it is significant that Orla accepted an invitation to my birthday party and she is coming here with Jules,' Giuseppe mused. 'I would be delighted if my step-children from my last two marriages were themselves to marry. But what would please me most, Torre, is if *you* would choose a wife and provide an heir.'

Torre stifled his impatience and headed towards the door, keen to avoid a discussion with his father about the fact that at nearly thirty-four he was still unmarried. His single status was something he intended to continue for many more years. But he understood that a recent health scare had focused Giuseppe's attention on the future of the family's construction company Afonso Romano Construzione—known as ARC. Torre knew that his father was desperate for him to have an heir to secure the leadership of the company, and he supposed that one day he would have to do his duty and marry a woman who shared similar interests and values to him in order to have a family of his own. But, unlike his father, he had no intention of being led by his heart or his hormones.

Torre loved his father and respected his business acumen, which had helped to make ARC the biggest construction company in Italy, responsible for many of the country's civil and infrastructure works. But outside the boardroom Giuseppe's personal life had been less impressive. He had regularly been unfaithful to his second wife, Sandrine—Jules's mother—and his inability to resist the countless young women who were attracted to his wealth in the way that predatory sharks were attracted to blood had made Giuseppe an object of ridicule in the press.

Eight years ago the paparazzi's interest in Giuseppe's private life had become frenzied when he had fallen for an English former glamour model and Z-List celebrity Kimberly Connaught. Within months of meeting her, Giuseppe had divorced Sandrine and married Kimberly.

Not even Torre had been invited to his father's secret wedding, and the first time he'd met his new stepmother had been at the party Giuseppe had thrown to celebrate the marriage.

It had been obvious to Torre that his father's new wife was a gold-digger and he'd failed to understand how Giuseppe had been such a fool. But at the party that night he had met a red-haired witch in the guise of an angel and his arrogant belief that he was a better man than his father had come crashing down around him.

'I'm surprised that you are pleased about the possibility of a match between Jules and Orla,' he told Giuseppe. 'When I was in England a month ago there was speculation in many of the newspapers that she had been awarded a huge divorce settlement from her ex-husband. Apparently her marriage to a well-known sports star lasted for less than a year before she dumped him. It would seem that Orla has inherited her mother's gold-digger tendencies for marrying and divorcing rich men,' Torre said sardonically. 'If she has set her sights on Jules then God help him.'

'I don't believe much of what is printed in newspapers, and I certainly do not believe that Orla is interested in Jules's money.' Giuseppe looked closely at Torre when he gave a snort. 'I have noticed before when I've spoken about Orla that you seem to have a low opinion of her, and yet you say that you hardly remember her. Did something happen between the two of you years ago? I recall that Orla rushed back to England the day after the wedding party, ostensibly because she was due to start at university.'

'Of course nothing happened.' Torre gave a laugh that sounded too loud to his ears. He avoided his father's speculative gaze and shoved the image of Orla's slender beauty to a far corner of his mind. It was a constant irritation that he had been unable to completely eradicate his memories of her. Other women regularly came and went in his life without making an impact on him and he did not understand the restless feeling that had gripped him since he'd learned that Orla was coming to Amalfi.

'I'm merely concerned that Jules doesn't make a fool of himself over her. You know what a dreamer he is,' he said, striving for a casual tone. But as he strode out of the study he had the uncomfortable sense that Giuseppe's shrewd grey eyes had seen more than Torre wanted him to.

Damn it, he thought savagely. Damn *her*—the red-haired sorceress who had cast a spell on him that night eight years ago. Thank God he had come to his senses the next morning. Right now he had enough to deal with since his father had decided to retire and hand over the role of Joint Chairman and CEO of the company to him. Torre had always known that it was his destiny and he was determined to run ARC as successfully as his father and grandfather, Afonso, had done. But he had a passion for engineering, and after he had qualified as a civil engineer he had carved out a niche role for himself as an expert advisor and troubleshooter, visiting ARC construction projects around the world.

He enjoyed his job and the freedom it gave him, and he did not relish the restraints that would inevitably come with leadership. He acknowledged that he had a few nerves, too, at the prospect of filling his father's shoes. The last thing he needed was to meet Orla again and be reminded of the shameful lapse of judgement he had made eight years ago.

If his stepbrother had fallen for Orla's charms then good luck to him, Torre told himself. But his inexplicable black mood lingered and he felt a sudden need to get out of the house. Muttering a curse, he grabbed his car keys from the table in the hall and strode outside to where the current love of his life was parked on the driveway.

Unusually for midsummer there was little traffic on the Amalfi Drive. The road on the iconic stretch of Italian coastline hugged the steep cliffs between Sorrento and Salerno and was famous for its hairpin bends. Orla was glad Jules had said he would drive so that she could enjoy the spectacular view of the turquoise Tyrrhenian Sea far below.

But the tranquillity was suddenly shattered by the loud roar of a car coming up behind them. Glancing over her shoulder, she saw a red sports car gaining fast on the hire car they had collected at Naples airport. The engine screamed as the sports car overtook them on a steep bend. Orla held her breath, fearing it would crash through the railings at the side of the road and tumble over the edge of the cliff. In seconds the sports car had streaked past and was a flash of brash scarlet in the distance.

'There goes my stepbrother in his new toy,' Jules murmured. 'The latest model is reputed to be the quickest and most expensive car on the planet. Torre's twin passions in life are fast cars and women.'

Torre. Foreboding set like wet concrete in the pit of Orla's stomach. She had caught a glimpse of the driver of the open-topped sports car but there hadn't been enough time for her to recognise him. For a moment her nerve faltered and she was tempted to ask Jules to turn the car around and take her back to the airport. Take her anywhere as long as it was far away from Villa Romano and the man who had invaded her dreams for eight long years.

She firmed her jaw. Enough was enough, she told herself. She'd allowed a stupid mistake when she had spent one night with Torre to haunt her for too long. Everyone had regrets—and he was hers. But she was twenty-six, not the naïve eighteen-year-old who had scrambled back into her clothes and fled from his room with his mocking taunt that she was a gold-digger, like her mother, ringing in her ears.

In the intervening years she had survived an abusive marriage, and she would survive meeting Torre again and be stronger when she discovered—as she was confident she would—that all she had felt for him eight years ago had been an embarrassing teenage crush.

Ten minutes later, when they turned through the gates of Villa Romano the sports car was on the driveway but there was no sign of its owner, Orla noted thankfully. Jules parked the hire car and as Orla opened the passenger door the heat outside felt intense. She grabbed her wide-brimmed straw hat from the back seat, aware that her skin would burn—or, worse, freckle—if she spent any time in the sun. Her milky complexion and pale red hair were a legacy of her Irish heritage on her father's side—although on those precious visits to Liam Brogan's home on the wild, wet, west coast of Ireland when she'd been a child, sunburn had not been a problem, she remembered ruefully.

She gathered her long hair in one hand and piled it on top of her head before jamming the hat on. An evocative citrus scent from the lemon groves drifted on the slight breeze and mingled with the sweet fragrance of the honeysuckle that grew over the walls of the villa. On her first visit to the Amalfi Coast a month before her nineteenth birthday, Orla had fallen in love with the stunning scenery and intensity of colour—the vivid pink of the bougainvillea, the dark green of the elegant cypress trees and the cerulean blue of the sea surrounding the rocky headland where Villa Romano had stood for two hundred years.

Eight years ago she had come to Amalfi when her mother had become the third wife of Giuseppe Romano, the billionaire head of Italy's largest construction company. But the marriage—like most of Kimberley's marriages—had been short-lived and Orla had not been back to Villa Romano since her mother had returned to London and set about spending her divorce settlement.

Initially when she had received an invitation to Giuseppe's seventieth birthday party, she'd planned to invent an excuse for why she couldn't attend—knowing that Torre was bound to be there. But she had grown fond of her stepfather while her mother had been married to him. He had made her feel welcome at Villa Romano whenever she'd visited—only after she'd ascertained that Torre would not be at his father's home—and she had kept in touch with Giuseppe after he and her mother had divorced.

When Jules had suggested that she could travel to Amalfi with him, Orla had decided it was time she faced her nemesis. Meeting Torre again was something she needed to do so that she could put the past behind her and move on with her life.

A member of the villa's staff came down the steps to greet them and Jules strolled over to speak to the man while Orla looked around at the beautiful formal gardens.

'There seems to be some confusion over which rooms we have been allocated,' Jules told her when he returned to her side. 'Apparently some distant relatives of Giuseppe have arrived unexpectedly and Mario is not sure where to take our bags. I'll go and talk to the housekeeper and find out what's happening.'

'I'll join you inside in a minute. I want to stretch my legs after the journey.'

'All right, but keep in the shade. You are not used to the heat of the Italian sun, *chérie.*'

Orla smiled as she watched Jules walk back to the house. French by birth, he had a gentle Gaelic charm, and he had always been kind to her when she had visited her mother at Villa Romano, even though Kimberly had been the reason that Giuseppe had divorced his mother. Jules had continued to have a good relationship with his stepfather and six months ago he had been appointed chief accountant at the English branch of the Romano family's construction company. Orla lived in a studio flat not far from ARC UK's offices after she'd been forced to sell her mother's luxury apartment to pay off Kimberley's debts. She had got into the habit of meeting Jules for dinner once or twice a week and he had proved to be a good friend while she had struggled to cope with her mother's serious health problems.

At the same time Orla had been vilified in the tabloids for supposedly receiving a huge divorce settlement from her wealthy ex-husband. She had not asked for or received a penny from David, but that hadn't stopped the lurid newspaper headlines speculating on how much money she had 'earned' for ten months of marriage.

No, she was *not* going to think about the past, she ordered herself. She was finally free from David, and in many ways her disastrous marriage had made her stronger. Never again would she allow a man to control her as her ex-husband had done.

She strolled across the drive, inexplicably drawn towards the sports car. For the first time she understood how a car could be described as sexy. The sleek lines and scarlet bodywork demanded attention and the black leather interior was rampantly masculine. The car promised excitement and danger, and no doubt its owner would promise the same. But she did not want excitement, Orla reminded herself as she ran her hand over the sensuous curves of the vehicle.

She had thought that her marriage to David would give her the security she had craved all her life, but she had felt vulnerable and sometimes even afraid for her safety when he had been at the red wine. His mood could change in an instant, and for a long time she had thought she'd done something wrong that had triggered his outbursts of temper.

A flash of pain crossed her face and she instinctively lifted her hand and traced her fingers over the slightly raised three-inch scar that ran from the edge of her eyebrow up to her hairline. She wore her hair parted on one side so that it covered the scar, and make-up disguised its redness. But it would always be there, an ugly reminder of why she dared not trust her own judgement and would never trust a man again.

She had never told anyone about the mental and physical abuse she had been subjected to during her short, unhappy marriage to an English professional cricket player. David Keegan was popular with fans and the media for his affable nature on the cricket pitch and during post-match interviews. Orla was sure no one would believe that David had a drink problem, or that alcohol turned him into an aggressive monster.

The press had accused her of callously breaking David's heart and ruining his career when she had left him days before he had captained the England cricket team against Australia in the famous Ashes series. England had lost the series and David had lost his captaincy. In an interview he had blamed his heartbreak over his wife's desertion for his dire performance on the cricket pitch.

It had been easy to blame herself for the problems in their relationship when David had constantly undermined her confidence and made her believe she was as useless as he told her she was. It had taken a physical assault by him to bring her to her senses. She'd stopped pretending that everything was all right in her marriage and acknowledged that David had killed her feelings for him. If she had stayed with him, she'd been scared that the next time he hit her, he might *kill* her.

Taking back control of her life had been a hard process but Orla had discovered that she possessed a strong will and a gritty determination to survive. Returning to Villa Romano when she knew that Torre would be here was another step away from the girl with a head full of romantic dreams she had once been to the independent woman she was now.

'She's a beauty, isn't she?'

The voice from behind Orla was rich and dark like bitter-sweet chocolate laced with a hint of sardonic amusement that made her nerves jangle. She had heard the voice in her dreams countless times, but now it was real and her stomach lurched. She snatched her hand away from the car.

It was said that some men bought high-powered, piston-throbbing cars to compensate for their own inadequacies. The last time she had seen Torre he had been twenty-four or -five, but now he was in his early thirties, and he was probably losing his hair and gaining a paunch, she told herself.

Heartened by the thought, she spun round to face him and her heart slammed into her ribs as her eyes collided with his glittering grey gaze. She had an odd feeling that he had been staring at *her* rather than the car.

Eight years ago Torre had been impossibly handsome. With his perfectly symmetrical features and impeccably groomed image he could have been a male model in a glossy magazine. Now he was even more devastating than Orla's memories of him and his raw masculinity and smouldering sensuality evoked an incandescent heat in her blood.

Too late she realised that she should have heeded her instincts on the journey to Villa Romano and asked Jules to turn the car around. But she was *not* the awe-struck girl who had once believed in fairy-tales and seen Torre as her Prince Charming who would rescue her and keep her safe. She had learned the hard way that the only person who could protect her was herself and she was pleased that her voice sounded cool and crisp when she spoke.

'Hello, Torre. Jules said it was you who overtook us on the Amalfi road, driving like a lunatic.'

He smiled, revealing a flash of white teeth in his darkly tanned face. Orla felt heat unfurl in the pit of her stomach and with a sense of shock she recognised the coiling sensation low in her pelvis as desire. It had been so long since she had felt the heady sensation of sexual attraction. She'd believed that David had destroyed those feelings in the same way he had destroyed her pride and self-respect. It was disconcerting to discover that her libido was alive and fully functioning, and a disaster that it was Torre who had set her pulse hammering.

Memories pushed into her mind of his mouth on hers. The wild sweetness of their first kiss was etched indelibly on her soul. Eight years ago he had taken everything that she had offered him with a naivety that— looking back—made her want to weep. He had taken her innocence and then he'd crushed her as if she were an insect that he had ground beneath his heel.

'I admit I was driving fast but I know every twist and bend of the Amalfi road like the back of my hand,' Torre drawled as he strolled towards her. 'Besides, everyone needs a little danger to add spice to their life.' His grey eyes gleamed like polished steel. He halted in front of her, so close that Orla was afraid he would notice the erratic thud of the pulse at the base of her throat, and she instinctively lifted her hand and played nervously with the gold chain she wore around her neck.

'I don't. I think it's stupid to take unnecessary risks.' She raised her chin so that she could look directly at his face and discovered that he was taller than she had remembered. Even though she was wearing three-inch heels, Torre towered over her. She wondered why she felt a need to challenge him when to do so was dangerous. It would be far more sensible to walk away from him. But she couldn't seem to move. Her feet refused to follow the command sent by her brain and she was so utterly mesmerised by him that she froze when he stretched his hand towards her and took off her sunglasses.

'Your eyes are the exact colour I remember them. Hazel, with flecks of olive-green,' he murmured.

She heard the uneven sound of her shallow breaths and was sure he must hear the loud thunder of her heart. For the past month, since she had accepted the invitation to Giuseppe's birthday party, Orla had prepared herself for the inevitable meeting with Torre. In her mind the scene had played out with her being cool and dismissive, while Torre was contrite and regretful that he had rejected her years ago.

But her body wasn't following the script. She felt dizzy and light-headed—which could be a reaction to the heat, she hastened to assure herself. More difficult to explain was the heaviness in her breasts and the tingling sensation of her nipples tightening into hard peaks that she prayed were not visible beneath her dress.

'Do you mind?' She welcomed her flare of temper as she snatched her sunglasses from his hand and slipped them back on. She felt safer with her eyes hidden behind the dark lenses. 'I'm surprised you remember the colour of my eyes. I remember very little about you from eight years ago.'

To her annoyance he did not appear to be bothered by her sharp retort and his smile widened into a grin that made Orla catch her breath. 'Then it is fortunate that we have this opportunity to become reacquainted,' he murmured.

'Why?' she asked bluntly. 'I *do* remember that you couldn't wait to see the back of me after we had spent the night together.'

Torre did not seem to hear her, and the dark intensity of his stare caused the coiling sensation inside her to tug harder, sharper so that she wanted to give in to a crazy impulse to step closer to him and press her pelvis up against his.

She licked her dry lips and the darting movement of her tongue seemed to fascinate him. His smile faded and something almost feral sharpened his features. 'You were lovely when you were eighteen,' he said in a harsh tone. 'But now… *Dio*—' his voice thickened '—you are astonishingly beautiful.'

Orla stared right back at him, unable to move, barely able to breathe. He filled her vision and she was as blinded by him as if she had looked directly at the sun. He looked like a fallen angel or maybe the devil incarnate. Either way, he exuded a simmering sex appeal that made her tremble deep inside.

In the years since she had last seen Torre, his so-perfect-he-could-have-been-airbrushed features had become harder and more rugged. The sculpted angles and planes of his face were softened slightly by the sensual curve of his lips. Orla guessed that the dark stubble on his square jaw would feel abrasive beneath her fingertips, but his almost black hair would, she was sure, feel like silk if she ran her hands through its thickness.

Around them the air was hot and still, thick with a fierce tension that threatened Orla's composure. She could not look away from Torre, from his mouth that was somehow much too close to hers, although she hadn't noticed him move.

'People can change,' he muttered half under his breath.

'What do you mean?' She wondered if she had misheard him or misunderstood what he'd said. Her brain wasn't functioning properly.

He stepped closer to her and her senses were immediately swamped by the heat that emanated from him. The spicy scent of his aftershave was evocatively familiar and she felt dizzy and strangely disconnected from reality.

'*Orla*,' Torre said in a low, urgent voice that rolled through her like thunder and created a storm inside her. Nothing had prepared her for the lightning bolt of sexual awareness that flared between them. She felt drawn to him as if there was an invisible cord around them that wound tighter and tighter, and her heart pounded as Torre angled his mouth over hers and his warm breath grazed her lips.

CHAPTER TWO

'I THOUGHT YOU were going to meet me inside, Orla.'

The sound of Jules's voice catapulted Orla back to her senses and with a gasp she jerked away from Torre. So much for her plan to act cool around him, she thought derisively. Within moments of meeting him again she had practically thrown herself at him. Thankfully Jules's interruption had stopped her from making a fool of herself.

'I couldn't find the housekeeper to ask where we will be sleeping so I left our cases in the guest cloakroom for now,' Jules said. 'Hello, Torre.' He shook hands with his stepbrother. 'It's good to see you.'

To Orla's surprise, Jules draped his arm around her shoulders. She knew it was nothing more than a friendly gesture, yet there was something oddly possessive about the way he drew her close against his side. She glanced at Torre and saw that his eyes had narrowed and his mouth had flattened into a thin line. For a few seconds his expression was unguarded, but perhaps she imagined that he looked furious because he smiled at Jules.

'It's good to see you, too,' Torre said evenly. 'Cousin Claudio and his family have arrived on a surprise visit, and as the other guest rooms at Villa Romano are being used, I told Giuseppe that you and Orla can stay at my house in Ravello.'

'No.' Orla flushed when she realised that she had spoken out loud. 'What I meant is thank you for your offer, but there won't be room for both of us to stay at your little cottage. I'll go to a local hotel.'

The idea of returning to the place where she had lost her virginity to Torre was unbearable. She did not want to be reminded of how he had undressed her in the moonlight before laying her down on his bed. The night she had spent in his arms had felt like a beautiful dream but the next morning it had turned into a nightmare.

In her mind she heard the icy condemnation in his voice as he had demanded to know why she hadn't told him that she was the daughter of his father's whore. 'Were you hoping to persuade me to marry you, in the same way that Kimberly connived to get my father to take leave of his good sense and marry her? I can see the attraction of mother and daughter both getting their greedy hands on the Romano fortune.' His cold contempt had sliced through Orla's heart.

He had looked cynical when she'd frantically denied that she had deliberately kept her identity a secret from him. Her stumbling explanation that she had her father's surname, Brogan, but Kimberly used the name of another of her ex-husbands had made Torre even more furious. He had ripped away the sheet that she had wrapped around her, and his eyes had blazed with fury as he'd stared at her naked body and the tell-tale red marks on her breasts and thighs caused by the rough stubble of his beard.

'You sacrificed your innocence in vain, *cara*,' he

had told her. 'My father has made himself a laughing stock by marrying an obvious gold-digger, but I have no intention of making the same mistake.'

Orla was jolted from her painful memories when Torre spoke again. 'I demolished the old cottage a few years ago and built a much larger house in its place. There is plenty of room at Casa Elisabetta. I doubt you'll find that any of the hotels on the Amalfi Coast have vacant rooms at the height of the summer season.'

'That's true,' Jules said. 'It's always busy here at this time of year.' He smiled at Orla. 'You'll like Ravello. It's a pretty little town and the views over the bay are fantastic.'

There was nothing she could do but agree to the new sleeping arrangements with quiet dignity, even though she wanted to stamp her feet like a toddler having a tantrum and refuse to go within a million miles of Torre's home. Even if she *could* find a hotel room, she would not be able to afford it, Orla acknowledged dismally. She was at the top of her overdraft limit and had maxed out her credit cards, paying for flights between London and Chicago to visit her mother.

'Good, that's settled.' Torre lifted his wrist to look at his watch and Orla's eyes were drawn to the black hairs that covered his muscular forearms. He was intensely masculine and so gorgeous that her stomach muscles clenched. She could not help wondering what would have happened if Jules had not interrupted them a few minutes ago. She was sure that Torre had been about to kiss her, and she tried to reassure herself that her common sense would have prevailed, and she would not have let him. Her eyes met his and she felt embarrassed that he had caught her staring at him. He gave her a mocking smile. 'We should go and find Giuseppe. Lunch is being served on the terrace.'

He walked behind her and Jules as they made their way along the gravel path that curved around the side of the house. Orla felt Torre's eyes burning into her back and she was suddenly conscious of how her dress clung to her bottom a little too lovingly. She had never noticed until now how the silky material felt sensuous against her thighs when she moved. Warmth curled through her and she was mortified when she felt a molten sensation between her legs.

She pulled away from Jules so that his arm fell from her shoulders. 'I'm not used to this heat,' she muttered as an excuse. 'I'm burning up.'

The path led round to the rear of the villa where a wide terrace was roofed by a wooden pergola covered in vines. The leaves formed a green canopy that provided shade from the fierce heat of the midday sun, and the vines were covered with clusters of green grapes that were starting to turn purple in colour as they began to ripen.

Orla counted twelve people sitting at the long trestle table. Giuseppe stood up to greet her. '*Benvenuto*, Orla. Welcome to Villa Romano. It has been too long since you last visited,' he said as he kissed her on both cheeks. He turned to Jules. 'Why have you waited so long to bring Orla back to Amalfi?'

Giuseppe began to introduce Orla to the members of his extended family. She smiled politely as she shook hands with his various relatives, but she was puzzled by his comment. Why had he expected Jules to bring her to Villa Romano before now? Giuseppe knew that she and Jules were friends but she felt an inexplicable sense of disquiet as she recalled the strangely secretive look that had passed between the two men. It was as if a situation was unfolding that she knew nothing about and yet she was in some way involved.

Her new sunglasses were pinching the bridge of her nose and she took them off and slipped them into her handbag before pulling off her straw hat so that her hair tumbled down her back. From behind her she heard a muffled growl and when she turned her head, her glance crashed into Torre's hard-as-steel gaze. Once again something tugged in the pit of her stomach. She felt dizzy. But this time she could not blame the bright intensity of the sun for the scalding heat that raced like molten lava through her veins.

She tore her eyes from him, but not before she'd seen his sardonic expression as he watched Jules put his hand on her waist to usher her over to two vacant seats at the table.

Forget Torre, Orla commanded herself. But it was impossible when he walked around to the other side of the table and sat down directly opposite her. A waiter offered her a choice of wine to drink with the meal but she opted for water instead. She had picked up an unpleasant vomiting virus a few days before coming to Amalfi and although the sickness had thankfully stopped, her stomach still felt delicate. In fact, she rarely drank alcohol but she ruefully acknowledged that the idea of slipping into a drunken stupor where she would not notice Torre, much less imagine his darkly tanned hands on her body, seemed infinitely preferable to staring at the tablecloth.

Memories from eight years ago crowded her mind. Her mother had acted like a newly crowned queen fol-

lowing her secret wedding to Giuseppe, Orla remembered. At the party the guest list had mainly comprised
Giuseppe's cosmopolitan friends from across Europe.
Most people had spoken English, and Orla had overheard their mocking comments speculating that Kimberly had married one of the richest men in Italy for
his money. She had felt embarrassed but thankfully no
one had taken any notice of her or seemed aware that
she was Kimberly Connaught's daughter.

Kimberly had spent the evening clinging to her new
husband and hadn't bothered to introduce Orla to any
of the other guests. Orla had been about to return to
her room, knowing that no one would miss her presence at the party, certainly not her mother. But she'd
felt an odd, prickling sensation between her shoulder-
blades that had compelled her to turn her head and look
across the room.

Her eyes had been riveted on the man who had taken
her breath away earlier in the day when she had arrived at Villa Romano with some of her mother's girlfriends from London. As she'd climbed out of the taxi
her attention had been drawn to the swimming pool that
could be seen from the driveway, and she had watched
the gorgeous hunk who had stepped out of the pool
and raked his hands through his wet hair. His honed,
muscular body had not gone unnoticed by her mother's
friends, but Orla hadn't admitted to them that she was
sexually inexperienced and had not understood most of
their lewd comments as they'd speculated on his prow-
ess as a lover.

'He's Giuseppe's son,' Kimberly had explained when
she'd sauntered down the steps of the villa and greeted
her friends with a great deal of air-kissing before cast-

ing a critical glance at Orla's jeans and tee shirt. 'Torre is a sexy beast, but he's so arrogant the way he looks down his nose at me as if I belong in the gutter. I guess he's mad because now that I'm married to his father I'll inherit all Giuseppe's money when he dies.'

At the party that evening Orla had stared at Torre Romano and supposed that he was her stepbrother. But that thought along with every other had flown from her mind when Torre had trapped her gaze and she'd felt scalding heat inside her as if an electrical current had shot through her body. She'd watched him stride across the room towards her, and the feral expression on his hard-boned face had warned her to turn and run.

It was a pity she had not listened to her instincts that day, Orla thought grimly. She picked at her plate of ricotta ravioli that had been served for a first course but her appetite was still poor after her recent gastric upset—although she suspected that Torre's brooding presence opposite her was responsible for the knot of tension in her stomach.

Around the table the conversation was mainly in Italian and Orla was heartened that she could follow most of what was said. She had learned Italian at school and had practised speaking it during her visits to Villa Romano while her mother had lived there. Now she hoped that being fluent in the language might help persuade Giuseppe to give her a job.

'You're very quiet, Orla.' Torre's deep-timbred voice jolted her from her thoughts and she looked up to find him watching her from beneath his heavy-lidded eyes. Now that she'd had time to get over the initial impact of seeing him again she was able to study him more objectively, but unfortunately he was no less devastating.

His cream shirt was open at the throat, and the sight of his darkly tanned skin and a few black chest hairs made the knot in her stomach tighten. He looked relaxed—the exact opposite of how she felt—and when he'd laughed at something Giuseppe had said a few moments ago the sound had made Orla think of molten honey.

He was waiting for her to reply. She quickly glanced at Jules for moral support and saw that he was deep in conversation with Giuseppe. 'I'm tired after the journey,' she said diffidently.

Torre's brows rose. 'It is a two-and-a-half-hour flight from London to Naples. I can't imagine you found the journey *that* arduous.'

His sarcasm stung. 'I didn't realise that I'm supposed to entertain you,' she said tightly. 'What do you want me to talk about?'

The gleam in his eyes told her that she had fallen straight into the trap he had set. Her temper fizzed and she felt a strong urge to fling the contents of the water jug at his smug face. Forcing herself to breathe deeply, she tried to rationalise her response to him.

It was a long time since she had felt angry. She had learned that the only way to deal with David's explosive temper had been to remain calm and try to mollify him. On the one occasion when she had attempted to stick up for herself he had physically assaulted her. Unconsciously she lifted her hand and ran her fingers over the scar above her eyebrow where a ring that David had been wearing had cut deep into her skin when he'd hit her. The wound had bled heavily and had required her to visit the accident and emergency department at the local hospital so that it could be stitched. Across the table she saw Torre's eyes follow the movement of her hand and she quickly lowered it to her lap.

'Why don't you start by telling me about yourself? Eight years ago I recall that we did not spend very much time talking,' he drawled.

Orla silently cursed her fair skin when she felt heat spread across her cheeks. Images flashed into her mind, of Torre sprawled on a bed, his body a symphony of sleek golden skin and honed muscles. When he had pulled her down on top of him, she'd marvelled at how hard his body had felt against her soft, feminine curves. She had never seen a naked man before and the sight of his arousal had made her apprehensive at first, but then he had kissed her and her doubts had been swept away by the onslaught of his fierce passion.

She swallowed hard, determined not to respond to his taunts. 'What do you want to know?'

He shrugged his wide shoulders but Orla wasn't fooled by his casual air. His eyes were focused intently on her in the way that a panther might watch its prey before springing to make a kill. 'What do you do for a living?'

Her heart sank as she wondered if Torre had read the stories that had appeared in some sections of the English press after she'd ended her marriage. She'd had to wait until she had lived apart from David for two years before the divorce proceedings had gone ahead. A month ago the decree absolute had been granted, but her relief that she was finally free from her abusive husband had turned to shocked dismay when the tabloids had labelled her a greedy gold-digger who had demanded and won a huge financial settlement. Public support had been very much for David, while comparisons had been drawn between Orla and her four-times-married mother, who had made a career out of marrying and divorcing rich men.

She stared at Torre and wished she could confound him by telling him that she had a successful career. It had been Giuseppe who had first inspired her interest in engineering, and eight years ago when she had started university she had switched from a maths degree to study civil engineering. She had found that designing and being involved in the construction process of roads, bridges and other vital infrastructure might not be a glamorous job but it allowed her to be creative and innovative with an opportunity to make real changes to people's lives. A trip to Africa organised by her university to take part in the construction of a fresh water supply and sanitation facilities in a rural area of Sierra Leone had reinforced her decision to become an engineer.

But her greatest regret was that she had not finished her degree. She had met David Keegan halfway through her final year of studying, and part of the course had involved her being sent on placements to civil engineering projects to gain practical experience. David had disliked her working in a predominantly male environment. In hindsight she could see that he had revealed signs of his obsessive and jealous nature before their wedding in Las Vegas three months after they had met in a bar where she had worked as a waitress to supplement her student grant.

She'd been flattered by the attention from a good-looking sports star and her romance with David had been a whirlwind affair. After they had married he had persuaded her to drop out of university so that she could travel with him when he played international matches with the England cricket team.

Orla smiled at the waiter who had replaced her un-eaten starter with a plate of seafood risotto. Unfortunately her appetite hadn't improved and her thoughts were still on the past.

It had always been her intention to go back to university to finish her studies and qualify as a civil engineer but by the end of her marriage her self-confidence had been in tatters. She'd left with nothing but a few of her clothes, none of which had been bought with David's money. Earning an income had been vital, but her only work experience was bar work or as an office assistant during her gap year after she'd left school.

The additional worry about her mother's medical bills had prompted her to take an intensive secretarial course, after which she had been offered a job as a secretary with a construction company, Mayall's. Her knowledge of civil engineering had proved useful and she had quickly been promoted to the role of PA to the company's director. However, she had been fired from her job when she'd had to take an extended period of time off to rush to her mother's hospital bedside in America. Since then she had been turned down for every job she'd applied for, and now her financial situation was at crisis point and her self-confidence had taken another battering.

Eight years ago Torre's rejection had made her feel worthless. He was still waiting now for her to reply to his question. 'I assume you do work,' he drawled, 'unless your living costs are funded by someone else.'

Orla looked across the table at him. He was so handsome that he made her heart clench, so arrogantly self-assured that her brief spurt of determination to stick up for herself withered and died. 'I don't have a job currently,' she said flatly.

His eyes gleamed like cold steel. 'And yet Giuseppe mentioned that you live in a highly sought-after area of London. How can you afford to live at an address in Chelsea when you do not work?'

'It's none of your business,' she said coolly. She had not told Giuseppe that she'd sold the luxurious apartment he had given her mother as part of the divorce settlement so that she could pay off some of Kimberly's debts.

Deep down, Orla was shaking at her temerity in answering Torre back, and she tensed, waiting for him to lose his temper as David had invariably done if she had ever disagreed with him. But he said nothing, and she could almost believe that she had seen a flicker of reluctant respect in his eyes.

The discovery that her mother had taken out a mortgage on the Chelsea apartment had been another blow. She had hoped to use the money from the sale to cover Kimberley's medical expenses at a hospital in Chicago where she had been receiving treatment ever since she had suffered a stroke that had almost killed her. But there was no point explaining the situation to Torre. He had made it clear that he despised her mother and Orla knew he would not feel any sympathy.

Jules finished his conversation with Giuseppe and turned his head towards her. 'You haven't eaten much. Are you feeling unwell again? That was a nasty virus you contracted last week.'

Jules was such a good friend. Orla gave him a grateful smile. 'I'm fine.'

Against her will, her eyes darted to Torre and his sardonic expression infuriated her. But Jules seemed oblivious to the simmering tension. He glanced across the table at Torre. 'You and Orla must have a lot to catch up on after eight years.'

'I was interested to know what job Orla does but she has informed me that she doesn't work,' Torre said drily.

'I hope she explained that what happened with her previous employer was not her fault.' Jules quickly sprang to her defence. He turned to Giuseppe. 'Orla is a very good secretary and she is ideally suitable for the position of PA to the audit manager of ARC UK, but her application was rejected by the managing director, Richard Fraser. I am certain that Orla would be an asset to the company if you would give her a chance to prove her worth.'

Orla felt uncomfortable when Giuseppe gave her a shrewd look. 'It is not a chairman's role to interfere with decisions made by senior executives, except in rare circumstances,' he murmured. 'I like Richard Fraser and respect his judgement. That said, I would like to help you, Orla. You are my stepdaughter and I am delighted that you wish to work for the company. But I am no longer in charge of ARC. I intend to make a formal announcement and give a press statement at the company's centenary party that I am stepping down from my role as joint Chairman and CEO in favour of my son. I began the legal process of handing the company over to Torre a few weeks ago while I was in hospital, suffering from pneumonia. My illness forced me to accept that I am getting older, and it is time for a younger man with more energy and new ideas to lead ARC into the future.'

Around the table everyone turned their heads to look at Giuseppe when he rose to his feet and picked up his wine glass. 'I would like to propose a toast to Torre. I am certain that under his leadership ARC will continue to flourish and expand.'

There was a scrape of chairs on the stone terrace as everyone stood up and raised their glasses. Orla murmured her congratulations, but her heart had plummeted when Giuseppe had made his announcement. She had let herself believe that she would be able to persuade her stepfather to give her a job at ARC UK. But Giuseppe, who had only ever been kind to her, had handed the company over to his son and heir—and Torre was as friendly towards her as a rattlesnake.

When everyone had resumed their seats, Jules leaned across the table and spoke to Torre. 'I'd appreciate it if you would intervene on Orla's behalf and tell Richard Fraser to offer her the job she applied for. If you read her CV you will see that she has the right qualifications.'

'I cannot promise anything. Recruitment is dealt with by HR,' Torre said smoothly. 'But I suppose I can spare five minutes to look at Orla's CV.'

She wanted to tell him not to bother. It would save them both time because she was damned sure that Torre would not give her a job. She didn't even want to be a PA. She did not enjoy office work but it was the only thing she was qualified to do. Even if she found the confidence to go back to university for the final year of her degree in civil engineering, she could not afford the fees or the lack of income while she studied. She *had* to have a job so that she could pay her mother's medical expenses, and she couldn't risk throwing away the tiny chance that Torre might employ her.

'I assume you have your CV with you?' he said.

'Yes.' She fished in her handbag and took out the document. Torre reached across the table to take it from her and their hands brushed. It had only been a fleeting touch of his skin against hers, but Orla caught her breath.

His mouth curled in a cynical smile that made her feel suddenly furious. What right did he have to look at her as if she had crawled out from beneath a rock? Her only crime had been to sleep with him. She had naively mistaken lust for something deeper, but love was an illusion, she thought bleakly. Eight years ago Torre had only wanted her body, but she had been a foolish eighteen-year-old and for one magical night she had believed in love at first sight. A few years later she had thought she loved David but he had treated her badly.

Once again her eyes were drawn to Torre and she found him watching her with an indefinable expression in his steel-grey gaze that sent confused signals down to the molten core of her, right *there* between her legs, so that she pressed her trembling thighs together. He *knew*, damn him, she thought as shame swept in a hot tide across her cheeks. He knew that she was fighting her awareness of him. Something in his smouldering gaze made her think that he was remembering how he had almost kissed her when he had found her alone on the driveway.

'Meet me in the library in twenty minutes to discuss your CV,' he said abruptly as he rose to his feet. 'If you can convince me that you have skills that would be useful to the company I will consider passing your folder over to HR.'

It wasn't exactly a ringing endorsement but at least he

hadn't dismissed her outright. 'Thank you.' She tensed when Jules placed his hand over hers where it was lying on the tablecloth.

'I promised you that everything would be all right, didn't I, *chérie?*'

Orla was conscious that Torre's eyes had narrowed and she flushed guiltily even though she had done nothing to feel guilty about. She wanted to snatch her hand back, certain that she hadn't imagined a possessive note in Jules's voice which left her feeling confused. It had been a mistake to come to Villa Romano, she thought as she watched Torre stride away. She had a sense of foreboding, a feeling that she was set on a dangerous path and there was no going back.

CHAPTER THREE

TORRE WAS AWARE of the moment Orla entered the library even though his back was facing the door and she made no sound. His skin tightened as he discerned the subtle scent of her perfume; a light, floral fragrance with notes of jasmine and something elusive that reminded him of a sultry, summer's night a long time ago.

Once, when his father had still been married to Kimberly, he'd arrived at Villa Romano from a business trip and learned that he had missed Orla by an hour. She had been in Amalfi to visit her mother but had left to catch a flight back to England. Torre had assured himself that he had no desire to meet Orla again. But when he had walked into the library—where, according to his father, Orla had preferred to spend most of her time, instead of lying on a sunbed by the pool and flicking through gossip magazines, which invariably was how her mother had occupied herself—he had inhaled the faint, lingering scent of her perfume and his body had clenched hard.

Now, years after that incident, he was once again standing in the library and his senses were tantalised by Orla's perfume. *Thank God* he hadn't kissed her earlier, Torre thought grimly. He could not rationalise the crazy impulse he'd felt to bundle her into his car and whisk her away to his house in Ravello.

He had admitted to himself that he had been mildly curious to see her again after so many years. But when he had found her standing next to his car he'd been unprepared for the fierce hunger that had clawed like a wild beast inside him as she'd turned around, a slender figure in a muted green dress made of a silky material that had caressed her small, high breasts and the soft curves of her hips. Her wide-brimmed hat had shaded her face, and her eyes had been hidden behind her sunglasses. The overall effect had been one of understated elegance, and in the sultry heat of an Italian summer's day she had looked as deliciously cool and refined as gin and tonic with ice, and as fragrant as an English rose.

Torre's breath had been knocked from his body by the force of his heart slamming against his ribs. In that instant he had forgotten who she was, or rather *what* she was. But in reality he *knew* that Orla had had her own agenda when she'd slept with him years ago and he was *certain* that she had traded her virginity in the expectation that he had been as gullible as his father, who had married her parasite of a mother.

It was fortunate that Jules had walked down the drive. His timely appearance had saved Torre from repeating the mistake he'd made in the past, when passion had overruled his good sense. He frowned as he thought of his stepbrother. He liked Jules, even though their personalities were diametrically opposite. Jules was far kinder than Torre would ever be and had inherited his unassuming nature from his mother.

Sandrine had become Torre's stepmother when he was ten, and she had to a large degree filled the gaping void inside him left by his mother's death when he was six years old. He had been unable to comprehend why his father had replaced gentle and gracious Sandrine with the avaricious trollop that was Kimberly Connaught. So, when Orla had revealed after he had spent the night with her that she was Kimberly's daughter, he had angrily accused her of duping him. He had been even more furious with himself because he'd fallen into the same honey trap as his father and allowed himself to be seduced by feminine wiles. Worst of all, Torre had felt a sense of guilt that he had in some way betrayed his stepmother's kindness by sleeping in the enemy's camp.

'Torre.'

He jerked his mind back to the present. Orla had obviously grown tired of waiting for him to notice her and he heard a faint click as she closed the library door. Her voice was clear and soft like a mountain stream and Torre felt as though a velvet-gloved hand had wrapped around his body. All through that damned lunch he had been unable to take his eyes off her and his stomach had rebelled at the idea of food when he'd wanted to assuage a different kind of hunger.

But he was *not* a callow youth riding high on a surfeit of hormones, he reminded himself. He did not allow anyone to threaten his self-control, especially not a woman who, according to press reports, was as mercenary as her mother. Torre breathed deeply before he swung round from the window to face Orla and scowled. Her cool composure infuriated him and made him want to disturb her the way she disturbed him.

How did she manage to look so goddamned innocent when he had definitive proof that she was not? he thought bitterly. He was halfway across the room before he could help himself, and it occurred to him that it was unwise to get close to her when he felt crazily out of control. But now it was too late and he halted in front of her, close enough that he saw a flicker of wariness, and something else—a startled awareness—in her eyes before her long lashes swept down and hid her expression.

He remembered how in the throes of passion the green flecks in her hazel eyes had darkened to olive. Her long, straight hair streamed down her back like a curtain of silk. Torre knew he should not feel inordinately pleased that she hadn't gone platinum blonde and her hair was its natural shade of rose-gold—the same colour as the sprinkling of tiny freckles on nose and cheeks that were noticeable against her porcelain skin. Quite simply he had never seen anything so lovely. She was a work of art, as fragile as a rare orchid and as exquisite as a precious jewel.

Thick, black anger clogged his throat as he acknowledged that he had never wanted any other woman as much as he wanted Orla. He hated himself for his inherent weakness that caused his blood to thunder through his veins and made him so hard it hurt.

'Why are you here?' he said harshly.

She looked genuinely puzzled. 'You told me to meet you in the library to discuss my CV.'

'I meant why have you come to Villa Romano?'

'You know why. Giuseppe invited me to his birthday celebrations.'

'He invited you to his last three birthdays. What made you accept an invitation to this one?'

'Seventy is a landmark birthday.' She shrugged. 'When Jules suggested that we could travel to Amalfi together it seemed like a good idea.'

'I bet it did.'

She frowned. 'What do you mean? Why did you say it in that sarcastic way? I don't understand.' Frustration edged into her voice and her eyes flashed with angry fire. *Good*, Torre thought. He wanted to ruffle her. Eight years ago she had been refreshingly unsophisticated—in fact, she'd been several years younger than he'd assumed, and he had been shocked when he'd learned that she had been eighteen. He had only discovered *how* inexperienced she'd been when she'd gasped and her body had gone rigid beneath him, but by then it had been too late for him to refuse the unasked-for gift of her virginity.

She must be twenty-six or -seven now, and he was surprised that appearance-wise she had not developed the sharp features and calculating expression of her mother. But she had lost her joyful spontaneity that had made her eyes sparkle, he thought with an irrational sense of loss. The grown-up Orla was reserved and aloof, a beautiful ice maiden with an untouchable air that could easily drive a man to distraction.

Torre strode back across the room and indicated to Orla to sit down on the chair in front of the desk. The obvious thing for him to do was to walk round and sit in the big leather chair facing her, but instead he leaned his hip against the desk and loomed over her so that she had to tilt her head to look up at him. 'I've read you CV,' he said, picking up the document lying on the desk. 'You seem to have the relevant secretarial qualifications but I cannot see any evidence that you have experience of working in an accounts department.'

'That's because I haven't worked in an accounts office before.'

'Then why did you apply to be a PA to the audit manager at ARC UK?'

'Secretarial duties are pretty much the same in any department,' she said stiffly. 'Jules told me about the vacancy in the accounts office where he works and suggested I apply for the job.'

It did not surprise Torre to hear that his stepbrother had tried to facilitate Orla being employed in the same department as him at ARC UK so that he could see her every day. 'You assumed that Jules would be able to influence the MD at the London office and persuade him to offer you the job.' Torre's tone was deceptively mild and he was fascinated by the rosy colour that ran up under her skin.

'I didn't assume anything,' she threw at him. But she quickly controlled her anger and the gleam of temper in her eyes dulled. Torre felt an urge to shake her, or kiss her; anything to shatter her serene expression, which irritated the hell out of him.

'Two things puzzle me. Firstly, I'm wondering why you are looking for a job when it was widely reported in the English press that you received a substantial divorce settlement from your ex-husband.'

She flinched and once again hectic colour ran along her delicate cheekbones. But she did not rise to his baiting and said flatly, 'A few totally untrue stories about my marriage break-up were printed in the tabloids. It's your problem if you choose to believe the lies written about me.'

'If the reports were untrue, why didn't you seek a retraction or sue the publications for libel?'

Her bitter laugh tugged on something raw inside Torre. 'I didn't receive any money from David. I didn't want anything from him. But ironically it meant that I couldn't afford the legal costs of taking action against the newspapers.'

He must be a gullible fool because he found himself wanting to believe her. 'So you applied for a job at ARC UK,' he said curtly. 'But the managing director turned you down. Does Jules know that you were sacked from your previous job at a company called Mayall's because of the amount of time you took off as sick leave? I phoned Richard Fraser to ask him why he rejected your application,' he said when she looked startled. 'He told me that he had spoken to the manager at Mayall's and discovered that you had been fired because of your appalling absence record.'

Orla stared resolutely down at her lap, and he felt a strong urge to capture her chin between his fingers and force her to look at him. 'I was going through a difficult time and I was unable to work because of...' her voice faltered—a clever piece of theatre, Torre thought cynically '...personal reasons that I'd rather not go into.'

'I'm sure Jules was very sympathetic when you told him your sob story. It must be useful for you to have a faithful lap dog constantly at your beck and call.'

She jerked her gaze up to his face, temper making those green flecks in her hazel eyes gleam. Torre felt a surge of satisfaction that he had finally jolted Orla back to life and got a reaction from her. A voice inside him mocked that his behaviour was like that of a small child seeking attention. He *wanted* Orla to notice him.

'That's not a nice way to speak about Jules,' she said huskily. 'He and I are friends...'

'He's in love with you. Any fool can see that.' Torre

rested his eyes on her flushed face. 'And you might be a lot of things, Orla, but you are not a fool.'

'Jules is *not* in love with me. You are *so* wrong.' She leapt to her feet, her breasts rising and falling jerkily. Now that she was standing, she was closer to Torre and trapped by the chair behind her knees. He watched the pulse hammering at the base of her throat and wanted to press his mouth to it, lick his way along her collarbone and taste her silken skin.

'Jules and I are *friends*. He's sweet and kind, but I don't suppose you can understand that it is perfectly possible for a man and woman to have a platonic relationship. You're so...*macho*.' She made it sound like an insult, like she was too refined to bear the idea of hard, raw masculinity. 'Not everything is about sex.'

'My stepbrother is a man, like any other man,' Torre said flatly. 'He wants to have sex with you and it's not hard to see why.'

He roamed his eyes over her, noting how her silk dress moulded the small, perfect mounds of her breasts with their jutting nipples. He could hear the harsh sound of his own breaths and the quickening of hers, and he saw the expression in her eyes change from anger to awareness that darkened those green flecks in her gaze to olive.

'At lunch I watched Jules panting over you like a dog when it catches the scent of a bitch on heat. He's besotted with you, and you give him just enough encouragement to keep him sniffing around you like a devoted puppy.'

The colour fled from her face, leaving her skin so pale it was almost translucent, and the fine blue lines of her veins were visible beneath the surface. 'You're disgusting.' Her voice shook slightly. 'What the hell gives you the right to talk to me like that?'

'I like and respect my stepbrother and I'm not going to sit back and watch him make a fool of himself over you when it's obvious what your game is.'

'And what is my *game*?' she snapped.

'The same game that you tried with me eight years ago. But even though you played your trump card and lost your virginity to me—presumably in the hope that I would marry you—I recognised that you had the same mercenary tendencies as your mother when I found you trying to steal some jewellery that had belonged to my mother.'

She made a frustrated sound. 'I explained that Kimberly had lent me some earrings that Giuseppe had given her. I wore them at the beginning of the party but I was scared of losing them and took them off and put them in my handbag until I could return them.'

Torre ignored the tremor in her voice and he was not fooled by her innocent victim act. The emerald earrings had been his mother's favourite items of jewellery. He remembered she had worn them even in the last days of her life when she had been so thin because of the cancer that she hadn't looked like his *mamma* any more.

He had been shocked and furious when Orla had dropped her bag and the earrings had fallen out. At the time he had refused to believe that his father had made a gift to his new wife of Elisabetta Romano's jewellery. But in the years since then he had discovered that Giuseppe had given away other items of his first wife's jewellery to several of his mistresses. Maybe his father *had* given the earrings to Kimberly, Torre brooded, feel-

ing a faint tug of guilt that he that he *might* have misjudged Orla. But even if she was telling the truth about
the earrings, she was no saint, he reminded himself.

'You had better success when you married a wealthy
English sports star,' he said coldly. 'But if your ex-husband had any sense he would have insisted on a pre-
nuptial agreement. So either you did not receive as big
a settlement as was reported in the press, or you've
spent the money. But luckily your *best friend* Jules is in
love with you and he'll do anything for you, including
trying to use his influence with Giuseppe to get you a
job at ARC UK. Unfortunately for you, my father has
handed the company over to me and I am not taken in
by you. I assume your ultimate goal is to marry Jules?
He's rich and he conveniently adores you. But there is
a problem with your plan.'

'You don't say?' Orla's eyes flashed with temper but
her voice was coolly mocking, challenging him and
loosening the tenuous threads of Torre's self-control
so that he felt undone. Heat roared inside him. Heat
and a terrible hunger that years of meaningless sexual
encounters had never assuaged. All this for a fragile
slip of a woman who wasn't even his type, he thought
with savage self-derision. He went for athletic, laid-
back blondes who liked their sex as uncomplicated as
he did. There was no reason why Orla, all big hazel-
green eyes, pale red hair and a tragic expression on
her too-pretty face, should tie him in knots. But, God
help him, she did.

He straightened up from where he had been leaning
against the desk and his body almost brushed against
hers.

'Your problem,' he told her softly, 'is that you are not

a very convincing actress. You freeze every time Jules gets close to you or shows you affection, and sooner or later the poor sod is going to realise that you don't want to have sex with him.'

'*I don't want to have sex with him*, you moron.' She put her hands on her hips, perhaps to stop herself from strangling him, Torre thought. But the subtle shift of her body brought her breasts closer to his chest and when he stared into her eyes he watched her pupils dilate. 'You're mistaken,' she choked. 'I have no plans to marry Jules.'

'I'm not mistaken about this.' Torre's control snapped and he gave in to the urge to touch her. *Finally*. He wrapped a strand of her long hair around his fingers and wrapped his other arm around her waist. 'You don't want to have sex with Jules, but you do want to have sex with me, don't you, *cara*?'

'You are *so* arrogant.' She glared at him, but she did not deny it, did not attempt to pull free from him. The green flecks in her hazel eyes gleamed with fiery brilliance, sending out a challenge that Torre could not resist. With a harsh groan he captured her mouth with his and kissed her, hard, and the fire inside him became an inferno.

Orla placed her hands on his chest, but instead of pushing him away, as he'd half expected her to do, she spread her fingers wide and slid her hands up to his shoulders while her lips parted beneath his. Her sweet breath filled his mouth and Torre felt a fierce sense of triumph when she kissed him with a hunger that matched his own—almost as if she had been starving for him for the past eight years, in the same way that he had felt an ache in his gut every time he'd thought about her.

He tangled one hand in her hair and pulled her slender body hard against him so that her pelvis was pressed up against the swollen, aching length of him. She was shaking, or maybe it was him. He was lost in the sweet ardency of her response as he kissed her again and again. And his control was gone, replaced by a desperate need that enraged him because he did not understand why he desired Orla with an all-consuming intensity that he had never felt for any other woman.

That thought infiltrated the sexual haze surrounding his mind and finally kicked his brain into functioning again. He did not *need* Orla, he told himself grimly. But just like eight years ago she had made him lose his iron grip on his control and with it his self-respect. He was weak like his father, a fool to his desire for a beautiful woman who he was damned sure was as avaricious as her mother.

He wrenched his mouth from hers, self-loathing congealing in the pit of his stomach as he stared at her softly swollen lips and hungered to taste them again. *Fool.* His nostrils flared as he sought to bring his traitorous body under control.

'The PA job at ARC UK has been filled by another applicant,' he told her curtly. 'But even if the position was still vacant I would not have given it to you, or any other job within the company.'

Orla blinked as if she had been jolted back to reality and the sultry heat in her eyes turned to wariness that made Torre's gut twist with something like regret. She stepped away from him and pushed her heavy swathe of hair back from her face with a hand that shook a little, he noted. But it did not detract him from what needed to be done.

'Take my advice and keep away from Jules. Move out of London and look for someone else to cast your spell on. God knows, you're beautiful enough that you'll have no trouble finding another puppy dog who'll fawn over you.'

He watched her throat work as she swallowed. 'You're wrong about Jules,' she whispered.

'He's a romantic and he thinks you are the princess in her ivory tower who he hopes to wake with a kiss,' Torre went on relentlessly. 'Little does he know that you are a mercenary tramp, and if he wants you, he'll have to pay for you. I'm curious—are you going to sell your body to him by degrees? How much will you charge for a kiss? For a feel of your breasts? Is your plan to make him wait until you've got the security of your name on the golden ticket otherwise known as a marriage certificate before you allow him between your legs?'

Torre was transfixed by the gleam of incandescent rage in her eyes and he was unprepared when she moved with surprising swiftness as she swung her hand up and slapped his cheek with a resounding crack.

The sound somehow jolted him out of the insanity that had gripped him since he had spotted Orla standing by his car. Maybe he had needed that slap to bring him to his senses, he conceded as he touched his face and felt the heat where she'd struck him.

'You might look breakable but you pack quite a punch,' he growled, aware with a flash of shame that he had gone too far.

His eyes narrowed on her face. She was so pale that he thought she was about to faint. He swore as he stretched out his arms to catch her. She drew an audible breath and flinched, and the flash of fear in her eyes shocked him. 'What the hell?'

'*I'm sorry, I'm sorry*—I can't believe I hit you.' She pressed her knuckles against her lips. Her eyes were wide with fright and her breath came in sharp bursts. 'I shouldn't have done it. I'm no better than him...'

'Than who?' Torre frowned when she pressed her lips together as if she regretted the words that had spilled from them.

'I'm sorry,' she said again in an appalled whisper. It crossed Torre's mind that Orla's strange reaction might be an act to gain his sympathy, but she was trembling, and the gamut of emotions that crossed her face were too raw not to be real.

'I deserved it,' he said curtly. Eight years ago she had made him lose control and made him feel less than the man he was determined to be. But the truth was that he couldn't blame Orla for *his* failure to live up to the high standard he had set himself. She might be a tramp willing to sell herself to a rich husband in return for financial security like her mother had done many times. Orla already had one failed marriage behind her. But perhaps her behaviour was not surprising when she'd been brought up to think that being a rich man's trophy wife was a good career move.

The shimmer of tears in her eyes evoked an unknown emotion in Torre that could have been tenderness if he had cared to examine it—which he didn't. His frown deepened when she tensed as if she was bracing herself to receive a blow. 'Orla—what are you afraid of?'

Instead of answering him, she spun round and he heard a crack as her knee collided with the edge of the chair. '*Dio*. Slow down,' he commanded as she dashed across the room. Torre caught up with her as she grabbed the door handle. He put his hand on her shoulder and she gave a thin cry like an animal in pain as she flattened herself against the door.

'*Don't.* Please, David...*don't...*'

CHAPTER FOUR

ORLA HEARD TORRE SWEAR.

Torre. Not David. She took a shuddering breath as the images in her mind of her ex-husband standing menacingly over her, his hand raised to strike her, slowly faded. She bit her lip, hoping she hadn't cried out David's name. For a few moments she had felt the same sickening fear in the pit of her stomach that she'd felt when David had cornered her in the bathroom. He had locked the door before he'd walked purposefully towards her, and she had sensed that he enjoyed her terror as much as he'd enjoyed physically hurting her. Ten months earlier he had promised to love her and protect her but, according to David, she had been a useless wife and deserved his black temper.

No one ever deserved to be physically or verbally attacked. Orla reminded herself of what the nurse in the A and E department had told her when she'd pretended that the cut above her eye had happened as a result of her tripping on some concrete steps in the garden. There was never an excuse for violence, the nurse had insisted when she'd given Orla a leaflet with information about a local women's refuge.

Her eyes flew to Torre's face and she gave a low

moan of distress when she saw the livid scarlet print of her hand on his cheek. Dear God, *she was no better than David.* She had been furious with Torre but that did not excuse her behaviour. Shame bit deep into her and she wanted to weep for the way her disastrous marriage had changed her into someone she no longer recognised as herself. She could not blame Torre if he retaliated. He loomed over her and she squeezed her eyes shut, steeling herself for him to hit her. But the blow never came, and when she raised her lashes she found him staring at her with an indefinable expression in his eyes.

He swore again but there was no aggression in his voice, and when he spoke it was in a low growl that somehow made the ache of misery inside her even worse. 'Are you afraid of *me*?' She saw disbelief and anger in his eyes but she had a feeling that his anger wasn't directed at her. 'What do think I'm going to do, *piccola*?'

He spoke quietly, as if he was trying not to scare her even more. Orla knew that the Italian word *piccola* meant 'little one'—and she simply unravelled. Tears filled her eyes and she could not stop them sliding down her cheeks. Her instincts told her that he would not hurt her. But her instincts had been wrong before and she hadn't guessed that David's outward charm had hidden his obsessive jealousy, she thought bleakly.

She did not know how to answer Torre. She hated herself for breaking down in front of him, but her tears kept falling and she buried her face in her hands so at least she would not see the contempt that she was sure would be reflected in his steely gaze.

He muttered something else in Italian but Orla was too caught up in her misery to make any sense of his words. She tensed when he slid his arm around her waist and she felt his other arm behind her knees, and then the room tilted as he lifted her and carried her over to a sofa beneath the window.

'Let go of me.' She struggled to get away from him, but he sat down and pulled her onto his lap, holding her firmly but without force. Unbelievably she felt him stroke her hair and his unexpected gentleness made her cry harder. She could not explain why she felt safe with Torre's arms around her. The steady thud of his heart beneath her ear as she rested her head on his chest soothed her ragged emotions. Gradually her panic receded and she drew a shaky breath as the storm calmed. She wiped her tears away with her hands and found her eyes drawn to Torre's face so close to hers. Too close for comfort.

'Feeling better?' he enquired, nothing in his deep voice to give her a clue to his thoughts.

'Yes, thank you.' She felt like she was made of glass and could easily shatter.

'Want to talk about it?'

'No.' Talk about her ex-husband's cruelty, or her shame that she had lashed out at Torre? Neither topic made for a conversation she wanted to have with him, now or ever. She attempted to slide off his knees but he subtly increased the pressure of his arms around her and she did not have the strength—mentally or physically—for another fight.

And so she sat still, hardly able to believe that Torre was holding her as if she was breakable, as if he hadn't said those horrible things to her and accused her of leading Jules on. Torre was wrong. Jules had never given any indication that he wanted more than the easy friendship they shared. She caught her lower lip between her teeth as she remembered that Jules's behaviour since they had arrived in Amalfi had been odd, and his possessive air *had* made her feel uneasy.

Once again she wished heartily that she hadn't come to Villa Romano to take part in Giuseppe's birthday celebrations. The party tomorrow evening was bound to evoke memories of the party eight years ago when she'd met Torre for the first time and fallen for him so hard and fast that she had believed she was in love with him.

'After the party to celebrate his seventieth birthday Giuseppe is going on a cruise,' Torre murmured. 'The change of scenery will be good for him and hopefully help him begin to enjoy his retirement.' He gave a wry smile. 'My father thinks that he is indestructible but he was seriously ill with pneumonia, and it's time he took things a little easier.'

Orla realised that Torre's light tone and casual conversation were a deliberate attempt to establish an air of normality after her emotional meltdown. She was grateful that he had not pushed her for an explanation. She took his lead and determinedly showed an interest in Giuseppe's travel plans. 'Where will the cruise ship visit?'

'Many of the Caribbean Islands. The ship stops in Jamaica, Barbados and Grenada, and I think St Kitts is on the itinerary.'

'It's a beautiful part of the world.'

'Have you been to the Caribbean?'

She hesitated. 'I had a holiday in Antigua.' Her voice was carefully unemotional. She did not explain that it was where she and David had spent their honeymoon

and she'd first glimpsed another side to her new husband's character. David had accused her of flirting with
one of the waiters at their hotel, she remembered. She
had denied it and they'd had an argument before David
had stormed out of the hotel. He'd been gone for hours
and she'd been frantic with worry when he'd finally returned. Somehow she'd found herself apologising even
though she'd done nothing wrong. It had been the beginning of ten terrible months when David's temper had
become increasingly volatile and she had never been
able to please him, however hard she'd tried.

'Where have you gone?' Torre's question pulled Orla
back to the present. Her cheek was still pressed against
his shirt and she heard the rumble of his voice deep in
his chest. Her other senses stirred to life so that she
was aware of the heat of his body and the spicy musk
of his aftershave, and tendrils of desire unfurled slowly
within her.

'I'm still here,' she murmured in a husky voice that
did not sound like her own as she pretended to take his
question literally. Beneath her bottom she felt Torre's
thigh muscles clench.

'Believe me, I am aware of that fact,' he said drily.
His chest lifted as if his breathing was suddenly con-
stricted but when he spoke it was still in that calm, un-
threatening way so that Orla relaxed. 'While Giuseppe
is away on the cruise for six weeks it is an opportunity
for vital renovation work to be carried out on Villa Romano.'

'What kind of renovation work?'

'The simple answer is that there is a problem with
the foundations. A few of the nearby trees are as old
as the house and their root systems drain any moisture

from the ground. In layman's terms, this has led to the house sinking as the ground it was built on shrinks.'

Orla nodded. 'Subsidence can be a major problem, especially with old buildings. Underpinning the villa to make the original foundations stronger will be a complicated job on such a big house.'

Torre's brows lifted. 'I'm surprised you know about subsidence and underpinning.'

For a moment she was tempted to tell him that she had completed three years of a four-year degree in civil engineering. But he might ask why she hadn't graduated, and she was too embarrassed to admit that she had given up the career she enjoyed for a man she'd thought she loved, only to have her self-confidence destroyed by a marriage made in hell.

She shrugged. 'When I worked as PA to the manager of the construction firm Mayall's I picked up some of the terminology.'

To her relief Torre did not ask her anything else, although his gaze continued to rest thoughtfully on her face. Sometimes his grey eyes were hard and bright like steel, but at other times, like now, they darkened and reminded Orla of woodsmoke. Suddenly she no longer felt relaxed as she heard the echo of his heartbeat beneath her ear thudding in time with her racing pulse.

Too late she realised she was in danger—not from Torre but from herself and her involuntary reaction to him. Her eyes were fixed on the expanse of his bronzed skin revealed where the top few buttons on his shirt were unfastened. Everything took on a dream-like quality. Hardly able to believe what she was doing, Orla put her hand on his skin and felt the heat of him and the intoxicating contrast of smooth satin overlaid with wiry black chest hairs. His ribcage lifted and fell unevenly but he made no move to stop her when she slid her fingers up the column of his throat and over the dark stubble shading his jaw.

Utterly absorbed by his male potency, she continued her exploration and traced the sensual shape of his lips with her fingertips. It felt unreal to be sitting on his lap with her body pressed up against the muscled strength of his. And if this wasn't real, if this was another of the daydreams about Torre that she'd had too often in the last eight years, then it did not matter if she angled her mouth beneath his in a blatant invitation.

The feral sound he made spiralled through her body, right down to the ache that pulsed insistently between her thighs. And with that molten heat came a sense of relief, a fierce joy that David had not taken everything and destroyed her femininity, as she'd feared. The tendrils of desire blossomed into something urgent and intense, a need she had *never* felt this strongly with her ex-husband, she admitted to herself. Not even in the early days of their relationship when David had been charming and she'd been flattered by his interest in her.

'You drive me insane,' Torre said roughly. His warm breath grazed her lips before he claimed her mouth and kissed her deep and slow, with a bone-shaking eroticism that stoked the fire in Orla's belly. He dipped his tongue between her lips and she welcomed the thrust of his bold exploration with a hunger that matched his. She knew he wanted her. The solid ridge of his arousal pressed into the cleft of her bottom with only the barrier of their clothes between them. Nothing existed but Torre and the fire that burned inside her so that she pressed down harder on his lap and heard him groan.

'I knew you were a witch the first time I saw you.'

His words were hoarse with sexual hunger, but they were an unwelcome intrusion that jolted her from a haze of sensual pleasure and forced her to accept the reality of the situation. Torre had made it clear that he despised her but that hadn't prevented her from throwing herself at him like the tramp he thought she was.

She pulled her mouth from his and it was the hardest thing she had ever done. Her body yearned to lean into his strength and burn in his fire. But she was not the naïve eighteen-year-old she had been the first time they'd met. Torre had broken her heart and it had taken her a long time to get over him. She had married David soon after she'd heard from Giuseppe that Torre was engaged to the daughter of an Italian count. It was only now that she could see there was a connection between the two events, Orla thought as she slid off Torre's knees and stood up.

She quashed a sharp stab of disappointment when he did not try to stop her. *What kind of masochistic idiot was she?* He had hurt her once and undoubtedly he could hurt her again. She did not fear him in a physical sense. Something deep inside her knew with absolute certainty that Torre was an honourable man and he would never use his superior strength against someone smaller and weaker than himself. But she hadn't only given him her innocence eight years ago, she had given him her heart and soul, and she had never forgotten his scathing rejection.

'We shouldn't have done that.' She felt ashamed of how easily she had succumbed to his sorcery. And she was confused by her response to him. After David she had been understandably wary of men. But Torre had dismantled her defences—because she had wanted him to, she acknowledged. She wanted him as badly as she had done when she'd been an innocent girl of eighteen—maybe more—because she knew that their passion was electrifying.

Pride was her only defence against him. 'You had no right to kiss me,' she said angrily.

'It was the other way round, surely? You kissed me.' His lazy smile mocked her but she could not define the expression in his eyes—although when she remembered how she had wept in his arms she thought it might be compassion that darkened his gaze.

She did not want his pity. Shame coiled through her and without saying another word she spun round and marched over to the door with her head held high and the sound of his soft laughter in her ears.

Torre watched Orla step into the corridor and found himself wanting to go after her. He could not understand the sense of protectiveness he felt, or the urge he had to hold her in his arms and reassure her as he had done a few moments ago. Women like Orla and her mother did not need protection, he reminded himself. He had met plenty of their kind; women who relied on their beauty and sexual allure to attach themselves to rich men like leeches, only letting go once they had bled their victim dry.

Orla already had one divorce behind her. It was easy to understand why Jules had fallen for her ethereal loveliness but her sweet nature and hint of vulnerability were all a clever act—weren't they?

He walked over to the window, the restless ache that Orla evoked in him making him feel edgy and yet oddly alive, as if everything was in sharper focus. Eight years ago the sexual chemistry between them had been white hot, but his emotions had become more complicated when he had taken her to bed and been struck by her generosity and eagerness to please him. *Dio*, she had given him her virginity and made him feel like a king who ruled the world. The next morning, when he had discovered her identity, he had accused her of being a gold-digger like her mother—*because he had been glad of the excuse to send her away*, Torre acknowledged.

He'd been shocked at how she had undermined his self-control. When he had seen his mother's earrings in her bag, and Orla had explained that her mother was his father's gold-digger new wife, he had chosen to believe that she was as mercenary as Kimberly. Why else would she have gifted him her innocence if not because she'd hoped he would put a wedding ring on her finger? He had refused to entertain the possibility that she was not a scheming fortune hunter and he hadn't stopped her when she had fled from his room. Later he had learned from Giuseppe that she had left Amalfi that same day.

Just because Orla had shown a vulnerable side to her when she'd had some sort of emotional breakdown a few moments ago, it did not mean that he had been wrong about her years ago, Torre told himself. He frowned as he recalled the fearful expression in her eyes when he had followed her across the room after she had slapped him. He certainly had not been about to retaliate, but she had clearly expected him to—which seemed to suggest that she had experienced violence from someone in her past.

He shoved a hand through his hair as he strode back over to the desk and picked up Orla's CV. His common sense told him that after Giuseppe's birthday party was over there was no reason for him to have anything more to do with her. But she had insisted that she wanted to work, and if he offered her a job it would give him a chance to find out if she really did only want friendship with his stepbrother, or if she was lining Jules up to be her next rich husband. It would be interesting to discover who the real Orla Brogan was, Torre brooded.

CHAPTER FIVE

ORLA CLIMBED OUT of the pool and walked over to where Jules was lying on a sun lounger. Usually she found that swimming allowed her to clear her mind. She had lost count of how many laps of the pool she had swum, but all that hard physical exercise had been in vain because Torre still dominated her thoughts.

The late afternoon sun blazed down from a cloudless sky and she moved a lounger into the shade of a parasol. 'I remember a few years ago Giuseppe told me that Torre had become engaged,' she said to Jules, trying to sound casual. 'Why didn't he marry his fiancée?'

Jules put down the book he had been reading. 'He was engaged to a beautiful Italian girl called Marisa Valetti but she called off the wedding. Torre never said why she'd decided not to marry him, but it's my belief that he has never got over Marisa. Giuseppe is always on at Torre to find a wife and produce an heir, but although he has plenty of mistresses he doesn't appear to be interested in settling down.'

After a moment Jules said diffidently, 'Did something happen between you and Torre years ago?'

'What do you mean?'

He shrugged. 'I noticed that he kept looking at you during lunch as if he is interested in you.'

Orla hesitated. She had wondered if Torre might have told his stepbrother about how she had behaved like a slut when they had met years ago, but Jules clearly knew nothing of her night of shame.

Jules had been his usual friendly self while they had spent the afternoon lazing by the pool and he hadn't given any indication that he was in love with her. It had been Torre who had put the idea into her head, probably because he wanted to spoil her friendship with Jules. Torre had made it plain that he did not trust her motives, she thought grimly.

'Eight years ago Torre despised my mother for being a gold-digger who had married his father for money, and his opinion of me was no better.'

'Why did he think badly of you? You had no influence on your mother's behaviour.'

'I suppose I was tainted by association,' Orla said flatly. In fact, she had often wondered why Torre had been so furious when he'd discovered that she was Kimberly's daughter. He had accused her of deliberately deceiving him. But the truth was that he had taken her breath away at the party when he'd walked across the room towards her, his eyes fixed on her face and a starkly possessive expression on his chiselled features. Her blood had thundered in her veins. She'd been unable to think and her tongue had tied itself in knots when he had halted in front of her.

Memories crowded her mind and she gave up trying to hold them back. She stretched out on the lounger and her mind flew back to that day…

* * *

Torre held out his hand. He was so tall—Orla guessed he must be three or four inches over six feet—and she had to tilt her head to look at his face.

'We have not had the pleasure of meeting before,' he said in a voice as rich and decadent as molten chocolate. 'I'm Torre Romano.'

He clasped her hand in his and she noted how pale her fingers were in contrast to his olive-gold skin. His dark tan suggested that he must spend a lot of time outside. The pads of his fingertips felt rough against her skin, and his broad shoulders and the defined musculature of his chest and abdomen visible through his fine white silk shirt were another sign that he did a physically demanding job. Orla remembered that her mother had said that Torre was a civil engineer.

He still retained his hold of her hand and she felt electricity shoot through her fingers and up her arm. 'And you are?' he murmured.

'Orla… Orla Brogan.'

'Orla,' he said softly. His husky accent made her name sound like a caress. 'You are English, I think, but I haven't heard that name before.'

'My father was Irish and he gave me his mother's name.' She flushed, feeling gauche. She had no idea why she'd told Torre such a personal fact. Her name was a precious link to the man she had loved more than anyone.

'You spoke of your father in the past tense. Does that mean…'

'He died when I was a child.'

'I understand how devastating it is to lose a parent,' he said gently. 'My mother died when I was six.'

She sensed he was surprised that he had spoken of his loss, and she wondered if he missed his mother as much as she still missed her father. But then Torre smiled and her head spun. 'Your father gave you a beautiful name, *Or*-la.' His accent elongated the first syllable. 'It is almost as beautiful as you.'

Was he flirting with her? She didn't know how to respond. Nothing had prepared her for a man like Torre—stunningly handsome, sexy and self-assured, he was a million miles away from the few boyfriends she'd dated. She knew that at nearly nineteen and still a virgin she was a late developer compared to most of her friends but she'd had an unsettled childhood, constantly moving around Europe as her mother flitted between lovers. Orla was determined that she did not want to rely on a man to keep her, like Kimberley had always done. Instead she focused on studying for her exams to get to university and had little time or interest in boyfriends.

But she was overwhelmed by Torre. He filled her senses and evoked a longing in her that she did not fully understand but it frightened her with its intensity. She tried to withdraw her hand from his, but he subtly tightened his hold on her fingers and stroked his thumb over the pulse that was going crazy in her wrist.

'Your glass is empty. Can I get you another drink?'

She glanced across the room to where her mother's friends, who had been on the same flight as her from London to Italy, were attracting attention as they teetered on their high heels, almost falling out of their low-cut dresses. They had been drinking champagne all afternoon while they'd helped Kimberly to get ready for the party and Orla had been dispatched on numerous errands.

She looked back at Torre. 'Actually, I was just about to go up to my room.'

He looked surprised. 'I did not realise that you are staying here at Villa Romano. How haven't I seen you before now?'

'I only arrived today, and I've been busy running around after Kimberly.' Ever since she was a young child Orla had been encouraged to use her mother's first name rather than call her 'Mum'.

Torre's face darkened at the mention of Kimberly. 'Oh, you are one of her retinue of assistants, are you? I had the pleasure of meeting my new stepmother earlier,' he said sardonically. 'God knows why my father has married an avaricious trollop like Kimberly Connaught. It's quite obvious that she married him for his money. I can spot a gold-digger when I meet one.' His voice was heavy with cynicism.

'I...' Orla hesitated, afraid that if she told him Kimberly was her mother he might feel embarrassed that he had been rude about her. And in truth she was embarrassed by her mother.

He smiled again and she forgot everything as she stared at him and thought how unbelievably gorgeous he was.

'Don't go,' he murmured. 'Will you dance with me?'

He led her from the crowded room outside to the terrace where music drifted through the open French doors. She went helplessly into his arms and when he drew her against his big, hard body she could not disguise the tremor that ran through her. His grey eyes were soft, like woodsmoke, as he muttered something in Italian. She stared back at him, unable to move, unable to deny him when he bent his head towards her and claimed her mouth.

His kiss was like nothing she had ever experienced before. And there in the moonlight, beneath a velvet night sky pinpricked with diamond stars, he exploded in her heart. There was no other way to describe the fierce connection she felt with him.

He lifted his mouth from hers and smiled at her low moan of protest. 'I think you must be a witch disguised as an angel, Orla,' he said hoarsely. 'Will you come with me?'

She did not even ask where he was taking her when he drove her away from Villa Romano. The twisting road climbed higher and higher until he stopped the car outside a quaint old farmhouse that seemed to cling to the edge of the cliff. Far below, the huge white orb of the moon was reflected on the sea.

'One day I plan to build myself a new, modern villa here,' Torre said when he took her hand and led her into the farmhouse. But she barely noticed her surroundings. She was blinded by him, made dizzy by his masculine beauty, and she was shaken by her reaction to him. For the first time in her life she felt the burning heat of desire, and he must have seen something in her eyes; an invitation, a hunger that was reflected in his smoke-soft grey gaze so that when he drew her towards him, she leaned against him and made no demur when he swept her up into his arms and carried her up the narrow staircase to his bedroom…

'*Orla*, you're not asleep, are you? I…want to talk to you about something.'

Jules's voice pulled Orla from the past and she

opened her eyes to find him looking at her. He seemed strangely tense, she noted.

'Talk to me about what?'

He did not reply and when she followed his gaze across the pool terrace she saw Giuseppe walk across the tiled floor and sit down at a table shaded by a parasol. Torre accompanied his father, and Orla's heart missed a beat when he looked over at her. His eyes were hidden behind his sunglasses but she sensed that his gaze roamed over her green one-piece swimsuit as if he were mentally stripping her.

She was suddenly supremely aware of her body. Her breasts felt heavy and she did not need to glance down to know that the hard points of her nipples were visible beneath her clingy swimsuit. The sun felt hot on her back and her hair, which she had tied in a long braid, felt heavy lying across one shoulder. She could not stop herself from staring at Torre and once again her mind was flooded with memories...

She had borrowed a dress from her mother to wear to the party, after Kimberly had said she couldn't wear her jeans when the other guests would be dressed in haute couture. Most of Kimberly's clothes had been too revealing for Orla's taste, but she'd found one dress of deep green silk with narrow shoulder straps and a slim skirt that fell to just above her knees. She'd twisted her hair into a loose chignon, and refused her mother's offer of high-heeled sandals in favour of her own flat ballet pumps. Kimberly had also lent her a pair of emerald earrings that had apparently been a gift to her from Giuseppe, but Orla had been so afraid of losing one that she'd taken them off and put them in her evening purse.

She had never taken much interest in her appearance before, but when Torre set her down on her feet in his bedroom and simply looked at her as if he could hardly believe she was real, she felt a heady sense of feminine triumph. Slowly he drew the straps of her dress down her arms and bared her breasts. The harsh sound of his breath catching in his throat made something tug hard in the pit of her stomach. 'You are the most beautiful creature I have ever seen,' he said hoarsely.

She trembled then, made weak by the desire that turned his eyes to molten silver. And when he touched her, stroked his hands over her breasts and rubbed his thumbs over her nipples, the sensations he created were so exquisite that she shivered. '*Bellissima*,' he murmured, before he bent his head and closed his lips around one straining nipple. The thin cry she gave was drowned out by the thunder of her heart as she went willingly to his bed.

'Orla.' Once again Jules's voice jerked Orla back to the present. 'Damn. It will have to wait until later,' he muttered.

She frowned. 'What will have to wait?'

'The conversation I was hoping to have with you.' He looked at her closely. 'Are you feeling all right? Your face is very pink.'

Orla was burning up, as memories of the night she had spent with Torre years ago collided with the reality that he was sitting a few feet away from her. She dared not look over at him again, but some sixth sense told her that he was as aware of her as she was of him.

'I'm hot,' she said, jumping up from the lounger. 'I'm going to have another swim.'

She ran across to the pool and dived in. The water was cold on her heated skin and she welcomed the sting of it as she swam length after length in an effort to alleviate the shameful flood of desire that made every muscle in her body ache. When she was finally exhausted she floated on her back for a while, delaying getting out of the pool in the hope that Torre might leave. But when she climbed up the steps, her heart sank as she saw that Jules had moved to sit at the table with his stepfather and stepbrother.

It would seem rude if she did not join them, but first she dragged a towel around her shoulders to hide her body's traitorous response to Torre before she walked over to join the men. Unfortunately the only vacant chair was next to Torre, and Jules and Giuseppe, who were sitting at the other side of the table, were deep in conversation.

'You are like a little fish,' Torre murmured when she sat down beside him.

She tensed as his sensual voice evoked a molten heat inside her. Somehow she managed to reply coolly, 'Covered in scales, you mean?'

His mouth crooked in a quick smile—almost as if he couldn't help himself. 'You know I didn't mean that. Your skin is silky smooth.' He stretched out his hand and stroked his fingers over her thigh. It was the lightest touch and barely lasted more than a few seconds, but Orla felt as though he had branded her and she couldn't control the betraying tremor that ran through her.

She glanced at Jules and Giuseppe. There was no reason for her to feel relieved that they hadn't noticed what had just happened. Nothing *had* happened, she told herself frustratedly. Torre teased her because he knew he would get a reaction from her. Thank God the towel she'd wrapped around her hid her painfully hard nipples, which were chafing against the wet material of her swimsuit.

'You are a strong swimmer despite your slight build,' he commented.

'When I was younger I belonged to a swimming club and I competed at district and national championships. I'd have loved to carry on training and perhaps even competed at Olympic level.'

'Why didn't you?' Torre sounded genuinely curious.

She shrugged. 'My mother's husband at the time had an indoor swimming pool in his house where I used to train. But after Kimberly left Roger Connaught for a Spanish lover, we moved to Madrid and then she had another boyfriend somewhere else—I don't remember where—but there wasn't an opportunity for me to join a swimming club because we moved around a lot.'

'How is your mother these days?' Giuseppe had finished talking to Jules and overheard Orla's remark. 'I am surprised that I have not seen photos of Kimberly or read about her in the newspapers recently,' he said somewhat drily.

Orla pictured her mother the last time she had visited her at the hospital in Chicago. Kimberly had been painfully thin and fragile following the devastating stroke which had had life-changing consequences. Orla had never been close to her mother but she could not help but feel desperately sorry for her situation. Kimberly's hospital bills were mounting daily, but Orla did not want to admit in front of Torre that her mother had long since spent the generous divorce settlement Giuseppe had given her. Neither would she ask Giuseppe for money to help pay for Kimberly's medical expenses. Her hope that Giuseppe might give her a job had been dashed now that Torre was in charge of ARC.

'Kimberly is in America at the moment,' she said noncommittally.

'How about you, Orla?' Giuseppe looked from her to his son. 'Torre, I understand that the job Orla applied for at ARC UK is no longer available. Are there any other positions within the company that might be suitable for her?'

'As a matter of fact, there is.'

Orla swung her startled gaze to Torre, frantically telling herself not to get her hopes up. There wouldn't really be a job. He was playing mind games with her.

'The role I have in mind is only temporary, but I'll view it as a trial and if you do well I might be able to find you a permanent position at ARC,' Torre told her smoothly. 'You will be working directly for me as my general assistant, and your first task will be to accompany me on a business trip to Dubai.'

'Surely you already have a PA?' She tried to hide her disappointment. He was the most senior executive in the company after Giuseppe, and soon to become CEO, and he was bound to have a personal assistant. She'd *known* that Torre would not seriously offer her a job.

'I have an excellent PA called Elaine—who is English, coincidentally. Elaine is based at ARC's headquarters in Rome, but she has a five-year-old son and an Italian husband and her family commitments mean that she does not travel abroad with me,' he explained.

'I also employ an assistant called Renzo who works

from my office in Naples and accompanies me when I visit construction projects in Italy and abroad. In his spare time Renzo is a keen cyclist, but he recently fell off his bike during a race and sustained multiple fractures, meaning that he will be off work for two months. The Dubai trip is primarily so that I can attend the official opening of a skyscraper that ARC was commissioned to build. It will be a prestigious event with worldwide press coverage, and I anticipate it will be a good opportunity to promote the company and secure new commissions.

'Your experience as PA to the director of a building company will be useful, and you have already demonstrated that you have a good understanding of the construction industry.'

Orla searched Torre's face for signs that he was amusing himself by pretending to get her hopes up, and she wondered if he could sense her panic when it dawned on her that he was actually serious about her working for him as his assistant.

'We'll fly out tomorrow. You'll need an evening gown to wear to the evening reception but you can shop for a dress and anything else you need when we arrive in Dubai. I'll fill you in on everything you'll need to know during the flight.' His brows rose when Orla stared at him in stunned silence. 'Any questions?'

'Um…' She wanted to ask why he had decided to give her a chance when he knew she had been fired from her previous job, but her tongue seemed to be stuck to the roof of her mouth. She could not shake off a feeling of foreboding that Torre had an ulterior motive.

'I imagine you'll want to know what I am prepared to pay you,' he said drily. 'You will receive the same

salary as Renzo earns.' He named a figure that made
Orla want to do a dance of delight. The salary was more
than she had ever earned, and even though it would only
be for two months, it would allow her to pay some of
Kimberly's medical expenses.

Her relief was tempered by the knowledge that working as Torre's assistant would undoubtedly mean they
would spend a lot of time together. How on earth would
she cope with seeing him on a daily basis? Somehow
she would have to hide her awareness of him, she fret-
ted, and only realised she had been biting her lower lip
when she tasted blood in her mouth.

'Where will Orla be based for work after she has
been to Dubai with you?' Jules's terse voice caught her
attention and she wondered why he was frowning.

'Mainly at the Naples office.' Torre kept his eyes
fixed on Orla. 'But I have several trips abroad planned
before I officially take over as Chairman and CEO and
I will require you to travel with me,' he told her. 'Do
you have a problem with that?'

Her problem was *him*, or rather her reaction to him,
she thought grimly. Her heart was pounding simply
because she was sitting near him, but she was determined to ignore her inconvenient attraction to him. His
job offer was a lifeline and she would be a fool to turn
it down, especially as there was a chance that it might
lead to a permanent position if she could impress Torre
with her professionalism and show him she had a good
work ethic.

At her previous job she had taken sick leave so that
she could go to Chicago to be with her mother when
Kimberly's life had been in the balance following the
stroke. Orla's boss at Mayall's had been sympathetic

at first, but her lengthy periods of absence had caused difficulties for the company and she had not been surprised when she'd been fired.

She met Torre's steel-grey gaze. 'I don't have a problem,' she said with a calmness she did not feel. 'I appreciate your offer of a job and I assure you that I won't let you down.'

'You would be wise not to,' he said softly, and she wondered if she had imagined an inherent threat in his words. She felt like she had thrown herself into the lion's den, and for a few seconds she experienced a cowardly urge to retract her acceptance of his job offer.

She watched Torre help his father to his feet and the two men walked back to the house. Giuseppe was still frail after his recent illness and he leaned on his son for support. It was obvious that Torre cared about his father and was protective of him. Orla acknowledged that eight years ago her mother *had* married Giuseppe for his money and a few years later Kimberly had won a sizeable fortune in a divorce settlement that she had frittered away on a champagne lifestyle. But now Kimberly faced spending the rest of her life in a wheelchair without the specialist therapy that might enable her to walk again. In the past months Orla had grown closer to her mother and she had resolved to help her in any way that she could.

'You don't have to work for Torre,' Jules said when they were alone again. His voice was strangely tense.

Orla gave a helpless shrug. 'You know I need to earn money to pay for my mother's care but I haven't been able to find another job since I was sacked. What choice do I have but to take the temporary job Torre offered me?'

She was stunned when Jules moved closer to her and took her hand in his. 'I know I'm probably rushing things—but you could marry me and you will never have to worry about money again.'

CHAPTER SIX

TORRE FOUND ORLA outside on the terrace where the music and the jangle of voices of the party guests drifting through the open patio doors were muted. She was standing alone by the balustrade, a slight figure in a silvery-grey dress made of a gauzy material—chiffon, he believed was the name for it—that emphasised her ethereal beauty. Her pale red hair streamed down her back like a river of silk, and in the moonlight her arms and shoulders—bare except for the narrow straps of her dress—looked as though they were made of porcelain.

She had driven him to distraction all evening while he'd hosted a party in honour of his father's seventieth birthday. He'd dutifully chatted to his numerous relatives and other guests, but he could not recall any of his conversations because his attention had been on Orla. His temper had simmered as he'd watched her dancing with a steady stream of partners, and he'd barely managed to restrain himself from striding across the ballroom and dragging her away from his good-looking cousin Fabio. Every time the young man's hand had strayed from the base of her spine and rested on her shapely derriere, a feeling that came dangerously close to possessiveness had surged through Torre.

Thankfully the party was winding down. The few guests who remained in the ballroom were staying at Villa Romano, and Giuseppe had retired for the night, leaving Torre free to follow Orla outside.

She looked cool and collected, in contrast to the violent tumult of emotions that surged through him as he walked over to her. His hand-stitched Italian leather shoes made no sound on the stone terrace but she turned her head as he drew nearer to her, as if a sixth sense had alerted her to his presence. Something kicked hard in his gut when he saw the glimmer of tears on her face.

'Crying, Orla? That's a little melodramatic, don't you think?' he drawled, angered by the inexplicable urge he felt to draw her into his arms and simply hold her. It had been easier to ignore his damnable hunger for her when he'd believed she was as mercenary as her mother. Now he wasn't sure what to make of her, but recent events suggested he might have misjudged her. His conscience pricked uncomfortably and his voice was curt when he said, 'You don't want to marry Jules, so why the tears?'

She stiffened when he halted in front of her and her eyes flashed with angry fire that Torre preferred to her tragic expression, which he suspected was genuine.

'How do you know that Jules asked me to marry him? Did he tell you?'

'No. But something must have happened to make him miss Giuseppe's birthday party and rush back to London, supposedly for an urgent but unspecified reason. Giuseppe had been hinting before you arrived that Jules had lost his head over you. I made a calculated guess that Jules would propose to you when I offered you a job as my assistant that would take you away from England and him.'

'I feel awful.' There was a catch in Orla's voice. Torre did not know if her show of emotion was fake and she was the clever actress he had convinced himself for the past eight years that she was, or that she was genuinely upset over Jules. *That* thought stirred a corrosive feeling inside him that enraged him even further because jealousy was *not* an emotion he was familiar with.

'I honestly had no idea that Jules had romantic feelings for me,' she said in a low voice. 'I believed he and I were simply friends. And before you make another of your nasty comments, I *didn't* lead him on.' Her flash of temper caused that fascinating colour change of her eyes from light hazel to glittering green.

He shrugged. 'I admit that I expected you would accept Jules's marriage proposal. If you *had,* I would have told him that you slept with me eight years ago and when we kissed earlier today it was obvious that there is still a strong chemistry between us.'

The moonlight was bright enough for him to see colour sweep along her high cheekbones. 'Nothing exists between us except mutual loathing,' she said grittily. 'Why *do* you dislike me so much, Torre? My only crime was to make love with you, and no one regrets it more than I do. But I was young and naïve, and you...' She broke off and bit her lip, causing the smouldering embers inside Torre to blaze into fiery flames as he imagined covering her mouth with his and soothing her ravaged lip with his tongue. 'You took my breath away,' she whispered.

He shoved away the thought that she had done the same to him when he had seen her standing by his car earlier in the day. 'I can't deny that physically you were innocent,' he said harshly. 'But you knew what you were doing when you chose me as your first lover, although you took a risk by not telling me you were a virgin.'

'A risk in what way?'

'I regret that I was not as careful as I should have been when it was your first time. In my defence you allowed me to think you were sexually experienced. But you were as manipulative as your mother and you used your virginity as a bargaining chip.' Torre had convinced himself that it was true for eight years and he did not want to accept the possibility that he had been wrong about Orla because it would make his behaviour towards her unforgiveable.

'I was *eighteen*, for God's sake. I went to bed with you because I was stupid, but I didn't force you to have sex with me. You were not a victim any more than I was the scheming person you make me out to be.' Her breasts rose and fell swiftly. 'If I was a gold-digger, like you have accused me of being, I would have agreed to marry Jules. And, to be honest, marrying him would solve a lot of my problems,' she muttered. 'Surely the fact that I turned down his proposal is proof I don't deserve your contempt?'

He shrugged. 'Perhaps you rejected Jules because you have your sights on a richer prize. Me,' he elaborated, when she looked puzzled.

'Oh, no,' she said in a cold, brittle voice that for some peculiar reason made Torre feel like his insides had been scoured. 'I wouldn't marry *you* if my life depended on it.'

She went to push past him but he stepped closer to her, trapping her against the stone balustrade. The voice of his sanity demanded to know what he was doing. Why was he acting in a way that was so alien to his character? He knew himself to be self-contained and he kept a tight hold over his emotions—a trait that he suspected stemmed from losing his mother, whom he had adored, when he was a young boy. To everyone he met he gave the impression of being charming and amusing, although many of his business adversaries had discovered to their cost that his laid-back air hid an implacable determination to win every deal.

In every situation Torre was *always* in control of himself. The exception was when he was with Orla. He couldn't think straight when he was around her, and worse than that he did not care about anything other than his need to assuage his hunger for her that made him shake and made him *less* than the man he wanted to be.

His heart pounded as he inhaled the evocative scent of her perfume. 'I imagine your ex-husband regrets the expensive mistake he made when he married you.'

She stiffened, and for a split second Torre glimpsed the anguished expression in her eyes that he'd seen when they had been in the library and she had mentioned her ex-husband. There had been fear in her voice, he remembered. But why would she be afraid of David Keegan? Torre was not a cricket fan but he was aware that Keegan was regarded as something of a sporting legend in England and he was also a hugely popular television personality who used his celebrity status to raise money for several charities.

Torre refused to move when Orla put her hand on his chest and tried to push him away. His eyes narrowed on her face. 'What was that about in the library earlier?

Obviously I didn't appreciate being slapped by you, but you reacted as if you feared I would retaliate and strike you.' He frowned as he remembered how she had cowered from him like a whipped puppy. 'I can assure you I would never hit a woman, not even with extreme provocation,' he added drily.

She caught her lower lip between her teeth once more, and this time Torre could not prevent himself from gently rubbing his thumb pad over the place where she had bitten the tender flesh. He felt the faint tremble of her mouth and heard her breath catch in her throat. The temptation he felt to kiss her was almost overwhelming, but he could not forget the look of terror that had crossed her face in the library.

He frowned. 'Was your ex-husband ever violent to you?' However improbable it seemed, Orla had clearly been afraid of something from her past. 'You sounded like you were scared of him.'

'I'm not prepared to discuss my marriage,' she muttered. And then in a stronger voice that nevertheless shook betrayingly, 'I don't have to stand here and be interrogated by you.'

She made a frustrated sound when she tried to step past him and he used his body as a barricade to prevent her. 'I knew you weren't serious about employing me as your assistant,' she said flatly. 'You just admitted that you offered me the job in a deliberate attempt to force Jules to reveal that he wanted more than friendship with me. Poor Jules,' she whispered. 'He rushed off after I turned him down, but I feel that I should go and see him and explain that even though I'm not in love with him, I care about him as a friend.'

'He doesn't want to be your *friend*. And if you did

decide to marry him to appease your guilt you'd only hurt him more in the long run. You won't be able to hide the fact that you're bored by him. And at some point in the future you and I will become lovers, and Jules will feel more wretched than he does now.'

In the dark her eyes flashed with green fire. 'You are such an arrogant bastard,' she hissed. 'I've already told you I have no intention of accepting Jules's proposal. And—believe me—hell will freeze over before I'd make love with you again.'

Torre was tempted to prove her wrong. Her eyes were wide, the pupils so dilated that barely any irises showed. She was breathing fast, as if she'd been running, or as if she'd been astride him and riding him hard. The image in his mind of her slender body arched above him, her silky red hair falling onto his chest, had a predictable effect on him. His erection was instant and painfully hard and he was infuriated by his weakness for her, only *her*.

He knew he was no angel. He'd had countless mistresses and one failed engagement to gentle Marisa, who fortunately was now married to a man a whole lot better than him. Torre's guilt about his broken engagement was something else he preferred to blame Orla for, rather than himself.

'I don't know how to convince you that I am not like my mother,' Orla said in a fierce voice that sounded sincere. 'I value my independence, which is why I need to return to London so that I can continue to look for a job.'

'My offer for you to be my temporary assistant *was* serious,' he told her coolly. 'I have already had someone from HR draw up a contract stating the terms of your employment. Come with me now and you can sign the contract before I drive you to Ravello. One of the staff took your luggage to my house after you'd changed your dress for Giuseppe's party,' he explained as escorted her back inside the villa and into the library.

He took out the contract from a drawer in the desk and watched her skim through it before she signed it. For the first time since Orla had arrived in Amalfi and exploded into his life once more, Torre felt that he had regained control of the situation, and he could not deny a sense of satisfaction that for the next two months she would be at his command.

Torre had opened the roof of the car, and a warm breeze rippled through Orla's hair as they sped along the winding road that led up from the coast to Ravello. She had read in a travel guide that the picturesque town was situated more than three hundred metres above sea level, but even at this height she could smell the salty tang of the sea mingled with the scents of lemon and olive groves. Every time the car rounded a bend she glimpsed a view of the water with the silver moon reflected on its surface, and its tranquil beauty helped to soothe her jagged nerves.

Jules's proposal had been like a bolt from the blue and she felt guilty that she had misread their relationship. All she had wanted was friendship, but even Jules's odd behaviour since they had arrived at Villa Romano had not prepared her for the shock of him asking her to marry him. She hated that she had hurt his feelings and it certainly had not crossed her mind to accept his proposal so that she could be financially secure.

Anger burned inside her when she remembered Torre's outrageous taunt that *they* would be lovers at some time in the future. She glanced at him and her heart kicked against her ribs as she studied his far-too-handsome profile. No doubt he was used to having any woman he wanted simply by clicking his fingers. But not her, she vowed. She would *not* repeat the mistake she had made when she'd been eighteen and had fallen into his bed. Even though she wanted him, a little voice in her head taunted her.

Torre turned his head towards her and she flushed at being caught staring at him. His mouth curved into one of his killer, sexy smiles and when she jerked her head round to the front she heard him laugh softly, as if he knew of her confusion and the shameful longing that pooled hot and molten between her legs.

How could this be happening to her *again*? she wondered bleakly. Eight years ago she had made the exact same journey from Villa Romano to Torre's house in Ravello. It had been her last night of innocence—not just because she had given her virginity to him that night but the following morning, when Torre had accused her of being a gold-digger like her mother, she had stopped believing in fairy-tales. She'd slunk out of his house in her creased dress and her tangled hair betraying her energetic night, and by some miracle she'd found herself by a bus stop just as a bus heading to Amalfi had appeared.

Sitting on the bus, conscious of the curious glances she'd received from the other passengers, had been a defining moment in her life. She'd learned a valuable lesson that the princess in storybooks needed to learn to take care of herself rather than rely on finding a prince. In truth, she had finally grown up, Orla acknowledged with a wistful sigh as she ran her fingers over the slender gold chain around her neck that had been a gift from her father. She had adored Liam Brogan and his death when she'd been a little girl had been devastating. In hindsight she realised that she had looked for a man to put on a pedestal in place of her father.

She sensed that Torre glanced at her a couple more times, but she kept her eyes firmly focused ahead. 'Welcome to Casa Elisabetta,' he said a few minutes later when he turned the car through a gateway.

Orla could not hide her surprise as she stared at the futuristic-looking villa that stood in place of the cottage she remembered from before. The new building appeared to emerge from the towering cliffs behind it, and her first impression was that its construction was a fantastic example of civil engineering.

'It's not what I was expecting,' she murmured. The houses they had passed on the road were built of local stone and in a traditional style; pretty villas with arched windows and coloured shutters. In contrast, Torre's house was an ultra-modern design. The white walls were uncompromisingly square, with unusual angles and huge windows that must give stunning views over the bay. It was a bold and innovative building that clearly reflected its owner's personality, she thought.

'Elisabetta was your mother's name, wasn't it?' she asked as she followed him into the house.

'Yes.' He looked at her closely. 'I thought you did not remember anything about me?'

She flushed and said quickly, 'Are you going to show me around?'

The sleek, contemporary lines of the villa's structural design were repeated in the internal décor, Orla noted as she walked through the large open-plan living areas on the ground floor. Bi-folding glass doors opened onto a wide terrace where an infinity pool looked like a mirror in the silver light of the moon.

'The building sits perfectly in the landscape,' she said to Torre as she stood on the terrace and looked up at the house, which was built over four levels. 'Did you design it yourself?'

'I had a strong idea of what I wanted but my area of expertise is in structural engineering and I worked with an architect on the house's design.'

'I'm fascinated by your drainage system. It must have been a massive task to excavate through solid rock to lay the sanitation and water supply pipes.'

He was silent for a moment and looked slightly stunned before he gave a shout of laughter. 'You are the only woman I have brought to my house who is fascinated by my drains,' he said drily. 'Most women are interested in the soft furnishings and the colour of the cushions.'

Orla supposed that her comment must have sounded odd. She stared at him, transfixed by his wide smile and the amusement that gleamed in his eyes, and her lips curved upwards. 'Drains are an important element of a building's design and a lot more interesting than cushions in my opinion.'

'I agree.' He was still smiling and his eyes rested thoughtfully on her face. '*You* fascinate me,' he said softly.

She wondered if she should explain that she had studied civil engineering, hence her interest in the villa's construction. But he might ask why she hadn't completed the qualifications and she did not want to admit that David had persuaded her to drop out of university soon after she'd married him. She felt such a fool for allowing her ex-husband to control her but David had been manipulative and it was as if she had been brainwashed by him.

A feeling of deep sadness swept over Orla as she imagined what might have been if, instead of rejecting her in the past, Torre had fallen in love with her just as she had fallen in love with him. Perhaps she would have gained her engineering degree and they could have planned the design and construction of Casa Elisabetta together, sharing their knowledge and interest. Maybe there would be a child or two upstairs in the nursery, and she would spread her time between being a mother and working alongside Torre. In this make-believe world she was confident and self-assured and Torre was proud of her. Just as importantly, she was proud of herself.

The painful reality was that she had survived her abusive marriage but David had robbed her of her self-worth so that she doubted her capabilities. Why would a gorgeous, clever, talented man like Torre fall in love with her? Orla asked herself bleakly.

She dropped her gaze from his, unaware that her expressive face revealed her vulnerability. 'If you don't mind, I'd like to go to my room. It's been an eventful day.'

'Of course.' Torre was no longer smiling and his cool tone shattered the camaraderie that had briefly existed between them. 'Come with me. There are no staff at the villa at night,' he explained as he led her through the house and up two flights of stairs. 'A married couple Tomas and Silvia run the house for me and they live in a staff flat next door.'

Had Torre made the point that they were alone in

the villa for a reason? Orla wondered when he stopped in the corridor and opened a door into what was obviously a guest bedroom. She noted there was a lock on the door and resolved to use it.

'What a lovely room,' she murmured with genuine pleasure as she admired the décor of dove grey, white and pale blue.

Like the rest of the house, the room was modern and minimalist but it still managed to be comfortable and welcoming—unlike her host, she thought wryly when Torre bade her a curt goodnight and walked out, closing the door behind him with a sharp snap. Orla turned the key in the lock anyway, even though it was obvious that he could not wait to get away from her. How different his attitude had been when he had carried her upstairs to his bedroom in the old cottage. In his impatience to undress her, he had ripped her dress as he'd tugged the material away from her breasts and bared her to his burning gaze.

Ruthlessly she pushed the memories away and opened her suitcase. Before she'd left London she'd bought a new nightdress, thinking that it would be too hot in Amalfi to wear her pyjamas. The white satin chemise felt cool against her skin and the slide of the silky material across her breasts was sensual. Her traitorous mind wondered what Torre would think if he saw her in the chemise. Would he desire her?

Angry with her unruly thoughts, she marched into the en suite bathroom to brush her teeth and saw in the mirror the hectic colour on her cheeks. The hard points of her nipples jutted provocatively beneath the chemise. She had better get a grip on herself if she was going to survive working for Torre for the next two months, she thought grimly.

Her heart missed a beat when she noticed that her gold chain was missing. She lifted her hand to her neck to check if the chain had somehow become caught in her hair and then ran back into the bedroom and searched for it on the bedspread and carpet. It wasn't anywhere, and when she shook out the dress that she'd been wearing she still did not find it.

Stop panicking and think. She remembered that she'd run her fingers over the necklace when she had been in Torre's car, which meant that she hadn't lost it at Villa Romano. The car was the obvious place to look but she was loath to disturb Torre. Instead, she hurried downstairs and found his car keys on a table in the hall where she had seen him drop them.

There was no harm in checking inside his car without asking him, she decided as she opened the front door and walked across the drive. She cursed when the sharp gravel dug into the soles of her feet and wished she'd thought to slip on her slippers and dressing gown before she'd left her room. She pressed the button on the key fob to unlock the car and the vehicle's alarm activated. The noise was skull-splittingly loud and although she frantically pressed the lock button, the noise continued.

'What the hell are you doing?' Torre's voice was barely audible above the alarm. Orla spun round and her heart gave an annoying flip as she watched him walk down the steps of the house. He strode over to her, snatched the car keys from her fingers and seconds later the horrendous noise stopped.

'Were you trying to steal my car, or did you fancy taking it for a spin?' he growled.

His sarcasm made her want to grind her teeth. She tore her gaze from his bare chest covered in wiry black hairs that arrowed down over his flat abdomen and disappeared beneath the waistband of his grey sweatpants. 'Neither, of course,' she said tightly. 'In case you hadn't noticed, I'm wearing my nightdress.'

The moment the words left her lips she knew it had been the wrong thing to say. Scalding heat swept through her body from the tips of her ears down to her toes as Torre trailed his eyes over the ridiculous bit of satin that had been designed to be worn in bed—but not to sleep in. She expected him to make another sarcastic remark but he spoke in a curiously rough voice that made her stomach clench hard.

'I'd noticed. So what are you doing out here at midnight?'

'I've lost my necklace and I wanted to look for it in the car. I know I was wearing it when we drove here. I've searched in my bedroom but it's possible that the chain got caught somehow when I took my seat-belt off.'

He frowned. 'Couldn't you wait until the morning?'

'No, I need to find it now. I won't be able to sleep until I know it's safe.'

He muttered something uncomplimentary in Italian and Orla decided that now was not the time to remind him she could speak the language. 'I assume your necklace is valuable for you to be so concerned about it.'

'It's priceless. If you would unlock the car, I'll look for it and you can go back to bed.'

'I'll look,' he sounded impatient. 'Go back to the house and, for God's sake, put something on. You are a dangerous distraction.'

She could not look away from him and was stunned

by the stark hunger in his eyes. Her breath was trapped in her lungs and her feet refused to follow the command sent by her brain to move, as something feral flickered over his hard face.

'*Go*, Orla,' he said, and the barely suppressed savagery in his voice brought her to her senses so that she spun away from him and ran back into the house. But instead of returning to her room, she walked through the ground-floor rooms and outside to the terrace and pool area, feeling increasingly desperate when she failed to find her necklace.

Finally she gave up the search and went upstairs. Torre was in her room, leaning against the dressing table, and when Orla saw her chain dangling from his fingers relief poured through her. 'Oh, thank God. Where was it?'

'It had slipped down the back of the seat in the car.' He studied the necklace. 'You said it was valuable, but it's just a cheap trinket made of gold plate and the stones in the pendant are green glass, not real emeralds.'

'It's a four-leaf clover, which is a symbol of good luck in Irish folklore. The necklace is precious to me because my father gave it to me on my tenth birthday. It was the last time I ever saw him,' she said huskily. 'My parents divorced when I was a baby and I grew up with my mother in England, but I used to spend every summer with my father at his home in County Clare.'

'What happened to him?'

'He was a fisherman and one night a storm blew up when he was on a boat out at sea and he was swept overboard. The coastguard found his body two days later.'

Torre looked down at the necklace. 'The clasp is

worn. If you want to leave the chain with me I'll take it to a jeweller's and ask them to fit a new one.'

'Thank you, but I'll wear it for now.' Orla walked over to him and held out her hand for her necklace. 'I keep it on all the time, even in bed.'

Instead of giving her the necklace, he moved to stand behind her. 'Lift up your hair,' he murmured.

He was so close that she felt the heat of his body burn through her thin chemise. The spicy scent of his cologne assailed her senses and she could not prevent the betraying tremor that ran through her as she stared at their twin reflections in the dressing-table mirror. He was very tall compared to her and his olive-gold skin was dark in contrast to her creamy paleness. He shoved his thick swathe of hair off his brow. His face was drawn tight with desire that gave his hard-boned features a sharp edge, and his mouth was so utterly sensual that Orla felt something tug hard, deep in her pelvis.

She could not find the strength to defend herself against his potency as she gathered her long hair in her hand and held it up so that Torre could fix the chain around her neck. The brush of his fingers against her throat sent a shiver through her. He laughed softly and she felt his warm breath stir the tendrils of hair at her nape.

In the mirror she saw her nipples peak so that their outline was clearly visible beneath her chemise. Torre made a rough sound in his throat, and Orla's breath left her on a shuddering sigh when he bent his head and pressed his lips to the side of her neck. Molten heat flooded through her.

Time ceased to exist and the world stopped turning. She was conscious of nothing but the sensual brush of his mouth as he trailed kisses along her collarbone. She stared in the mirror and watched him slide his hands round to her breasts to stroke the hard points of her nipples through their satin covering. The sensation was beyond exquisite and she could not restrain a thin cry that betrayed her need.

His strong arms flexed around her, and before she knew what was happening he spun her round to face him and jerked her against him, one hand on the small of her back and the other tangled in her hair as he bent his head and claimed her mouth in a kiss that plundered her soul.

CHAPTER SEVEN

HE UNDRESSED HER in the moonlight, sliding the straps of her chemise down her arms and then peeling the satin away from her breasts.

'*Orla.*' There was something akin to desperation in Torre's voice, and the predatory look on his face made her tremble with a desperation of her own that she could not deny when her body betrayed her desire. Her breasts ached for his touch, and she gasped when he rolled her taut nipples between his fingers until she thought she would die from a surfeit of pleasure. It was too much, *he* was too much. A little voice in her head tried to remind her of how he had humiliated her years ago, but she was deaf to the warning, dazzled by his masculine beauty and his intoxicatingly hard body.

He lifted up a handful of her hair and spread it across her white throat. 'It's like amber silk,' he growled. 'You are perfect. So beautiful. And, God help me, I can't resist you.'

He put his hands on either side of her waist and lifted her up high so that her breasts were level with his face. 'Put your hands on my shoulders,' he ordered, and when she complied he drew one nipple into his mouth and sucked hard, sending starbursts of sensation shooting down to between her thighs. She wrapped her legs around his hips and wantonly rubbed her pelvis up against his. The harsh groan he gave rolled through her like thunder and something primitive stirred inside her, a need as old as time and as consuming as wildfire.

She had only ever felt this uncontrollable hunger for Torre. What did that say about her failed marriage? her conscience asked. Had her ex-husband somehow guessed what she had been unaware of until now—that her body, her *heart* belonged to another man, to *this* man? Her confused thoughts were driven from her mind by the pounding of her blood in her ears. She could hear the ragged sound of her breaths. Or was the harsh rasp the sound of Torre's uneven breathing?

She gasped as he transferred his mouth from one breast to the other and flicked his tongue across the tight nub at its centre. His hands gripped her bottom and he circled his hips against hers, making her aware of just how aroused he was as he carried her over to the bed and tipped her backwards so that she landed on the mattress. Orla watched him strip off his sweatpants and the sight of his powerful body turned her insides to liquid.

There was a sense of unreality about lying sprawled on the bed with Torre, naked and hugely aroused, standing over her. If she told herself that it was a dream like one of the many dreams she'd had about him then she might be able to forgive herself afterwards.

His eyes narrowed and the gleam of steel from beneath his black lashes sent a shiver of anticipation through her. There was only one way that this madness was going to end. She'd known it from the moment he had kissed her. In truth, she'd known it when he had found her standing by his car at Villa Romano, Orla admitted to herself.

She did not stop him when he pulled the top of her chemise down to her waist and then whipped the satin slip off completely with an impatience that made her heart thud. His eyes locked with hers as he hooked his fingers into the waistband of her matching satin knickers and tugged them down her legs. He stared down at her slender body he had bared and a nerve jumped in his cheek.

A tiny voice of sanity demanded that Orla should move *now,* before she did something she would one hundred per cent regret later. But her body had a mind of its own and it wanted everything that the fierce glitter in Torre's eyes promised he would give her.

He knelt on the bed and leaned forward so that his chest hairs brushed the sensitive tips of her breasts. With a low moan she curled her arms around his neck and tugged him closer still, parting her lips as he covered her mouth with his and kissed her with an urgency that matched hers. It was a crazy, feverish need, a desire so overwhelming that she was helpless in the path of the storm.

He pushed her legs apart and slipped his hand between her thighs, gently parting her to discover the slick heat of her arousal. She sighed and lifted her body towards him, and he gave a rough laugh that *ached* with sexual tension. The fierce purpose in his eyes made her tremble with desire.

'Do you like that?' he asked thickly as he pushed one finger, then two, into her and swirled them in an erotic dance that drove her to the edge of reason and left her speechless. 'I see that you do,' he murmured. But she was beyond caring that her eager response betrayed her need for him as she arched her hips and moved against his hand, gasping as the first flutters of her climax started deep inside her.

Frantically she pushed her hand between their bodies, seeking and finding him. Emboldened by the groan he gave, she curled her fingers around him and guided him closer so that he pressed against her sensitive flesh. Orla did not recognise the wanton creature she had become in Torre's arms. She would not have believed that she could be this *desperate* for sexual fulfilment—with him, only with him, she acknowledged as she pressed frantic kisses along his jaw. 'I want—'

'*Dio,* I know what you want.' His harsh voice sent a quiver through her and she knew that if there had been a moment to stop the speeding train and end this madness, that moment had gone. Torre lifted himself over her and supported his weight on his elbows and then he simply thrust into her, deep and hard. Even though she was ready for him, his forceful possession was a shock and she could not restrain a sharp cry.

Instantly he stopped and drew back a little, his shoulder muscles bunched and his body tense. 'Did I hurt you?'

'No.' Already her internal muscles were stretching to accommodate him. And it hadn't hurt, she had just been overwhelmed by the feeling that this was where she belonged. In Torre's arms, in his bed, their bodies connected in the most fundamental way. She felt him start to withdraw and wrapped her legs around his back. The movement tilted her hips and he swore softly as she drew him deeper inside her.

'*Piccola*—are you sure you want me to carry on?'

Instead of replying, she cupped his face in her hands and pulled his mouth down to hers to initiate a kiss that he quickly took command of, as he pushed his tongue between her lips and at the same time drove his shaft into her body. He set a fast rhythm, taking her higher with every stroke, every slick, hard thrust, while she clutched at the bed sheets and gloried in his devastating possession.

It couldn't last. The fluttering sensation deep in her pelvis grew stronger, sharper, her pleasure building as Torre took her higher, higher until she was shuddering on the brink. He paused, sweat beading his bronzed skin, and stared into her eyes.

'I want to watch you come,' he said thickly. And then he drove into her again and sent her hurtling over the edge. Her climax ripped through her, each exquisite spasm so intense that it seemed impossible she could withstand the pleasure of it. She heard him give a savage groan as he followed her into the ecstasy of release, and in the aftermath a sweet lassitude swept over and cocooned her from the harsh reality that she sensed was waiting to break her heart all over again.

Too soon, Torre rolled off her and lay flat on his back. His silence was ominous and Orla did not dare look at him as she silently mourned the loss of his warm body pressing down on hers.

'So much for self-control.' His grim voice catapulted her from the lingering haze of sensual pleasure and sent tendrils of shame coiling through her. 'I didn't use a condom.' He jerked upright and swung his legs over the side of the bed, keeping his back to her as if he could not bear to look at her. *'Dio.'* He raked both his hands through his hair and swore savagely. 'I have *never* failed to use protection when I've had casual sex with other women.'

'Don't worry about it, I'm on the Pill,' Orla said flatly. She did not know what hurt most; hearing Torre describe what they had just shared as casual sex or his reference to the other women he'd made love to. Except she would guess that love played no part in any of his sexual liaisons, including this one. 'I've haven't had a sexual relationship since my marriage ended more than two years ago,' she told him in a cool voice that betrayed none of her raw emotions.

He stood up and pulled on his sweatpants. His face when he finally turned towards her looked as if it had been carved from granite. 'So why did you have sex with me?' There was an indecipherable note in his voice—not anger, as Orla had expected, but something that she could almost believe was regret.

She sat up and crossed her arms over her breasts, aware that it was ridiculous to feel shy of her nakedness mere moments after she had begged—yes, *begged*, mocked a silent voice of shame—him to make love to her. 'I wanted you.' The simple honesty of her reply appeared to surprise him and his eyes narrowed, hiding his expression.

She sighed bitterly. 'I was a fool when I was eighteen and I'm a worse fool now. But what happened was not only my fault. What is your excuse, Torre? Why did you have sex with me if you despise me as much as you make out that you do?'

'I don't despise you,' he shocked her by saying. 'I think I made it abundantly clear just now that I desire you more than I have ever desired any other woman.'

She darted a glance at him, startled by his self-derisive tone. This was a Torre she did not know. Tension emanated from him and she sensed that he was not as in control of himself as he wanted her to believe.

'Obviously I can't work for you now,' she muttered. 'You will have to employ another assistant to go to Dubai with you and I'll fly home as soon as possible and start looking for another job.'

She expected him to agree that working closely together would be intolerable for both of them. But he said tersely, 'Like hell you will. There's not time for me to hire another assistant at short notice. The contract you signed included a financial penalty if you leave before the two-month period of your employment finishes, or if you take more than a reasonable amount of sick leave,' he reminded her.

He strode over to the door and pulled it open, but before he stepped into the corridor he paused and glanced back at her, and his face softened slightly as he watched her pull her chemise over her head. Orla looked down and cursed beneath her breath when she realised that in her haste to cover herself she had put the chemise on back to front.

'We will be flying to Dubai on the company's private jet,' he said quietly. 'You will need to be ready to leave at eight.' He checked his watch. 'That's in six hours. I suggest you get some sleep.'

He stepped into the corridor and closed her bedroom door behind him. Orla immediately ran across the room and turned the key in the lock. But of course it was too late and the damage had been done, she thought bleakly. She could smell Torre's male scent on her skin, and the unmistakable scent of sex taunted her so that she hurried into the bathroom and stepped into the shower to try and scrub the shameful evidence of her stupidity from her body.

Qasr Jameel was the newest and most stunning jewel in Dubai's crown and the tallest building in the world. The skyscraper incorporated a six-star luxury hotel, a vast shopping complex, restaurants and numerous leisure facilities, as well as glass observation decks that offered spectacular views of the city. The English translation of the tower's name was Beautiful Palace and no expense had been spared on its construction or the internal décor and fitments. Several prominent members of Dubai's royal family would be at the party this evening to celebrate the official opening of the building.

From his viewpoint on the balcony of the Presidential Suite on the seventy-third floor Torre looked down at the stream of car headlights on the city's highways, glittering like golden jewels. The tower had been designed by a renowned Swedish architect and the developers—made up of a consortium of sheikhs—had commissioned ARC to build it. Qasr Jameel was a feat of exceptional civil engineering and the construction project had been highly complex. Torre was proud that under his leadership it had been completed on time and within budget. Tonight should be his chance to celebrate and reflect that ARC had proved it was a world leader in the construction industry.

But his pride in his professional achievements was not mirrored in his private life, and his thoughts were centred on the woman who had shattered his self-control *again*.

How the hell could he have been such a fool? Eight years ago his uncontrollable desire for Orla had diminished him in his own eyes. He had vowed that he would never be so weak again, and in truth none of his mistresses since had tested his self-restraint and his affairs had always been on his terms.

But the moment he had seen Orla at Villa Ravello everything had blown up in his face and he had been powerless to resist her. In his mind he pictured her lying beneath him, her slender limbs wrapped around him and her red-gold hair spread across the pillows. He recalled the flush of sexual heat on her pretty face and her pale breasts tipped with rose that hardened beneath his tongue.

'*Dio*,' he swore beneath his breath as his body clenched hard. He questioned again why he had brought her to Dubai. Despite what he'd told her, he *could* have found another assistant and released Orla from her contract. But it had occurred to him that a sure-fire way to end his fascination with her was to spend every day of the next two months working closely with her and have her in his bed every night. Boredom would replace his inconvenient desire for her, and then he would walk away and finally be able to forget about her. That was why he had insisted that she should occupy the second bedroom in his hotel suite, giving the excuse that he required her to be on hand should he want to work late.

He checked his watch. The party was due to begin at eight o'clock and they needed to be in the ballroom before the royal deputation arrived. Torre had not seen Orla all afternoon after he'd sent her to buy an evening gown and told her to charge it to his personal credit card. Puzzlingly, when he'd checked his account on-line the credit card had not been used.

He wondered if he should knock on her bedroom door and remind her of the time. A voice from behind him made him turn away from the window.

'I understand that there will be international press coverage of the tower's official opening,' Franco Belucci, the chief operations officer of the company, commented. 'It will be excellent publicity for us, and will put ARC's name in the record books because the height of the spire on top of Qasr Jameel makes the building a metre higher than the previous highest building in the world.'

'I doubt it will hold the title for long,' Torre said drily. 'There are already plans to build a taller tower in Bahrain. The CEO of the development company behind the new venture will be at tonight's party, and it will be a good opportunity to make an informal sales pitch ahead of our formal bid to win the commission to build the structure.'

Torre sensed that Orla had entered the sitting room, although her footsteps made no sound on the thick carpet. He looked over at her and was surprised that the sound of his heart colliding violently with his rib cage was not audible to the man standing beside him.

She was wearing a long, midnight-blue gown that showed off her slender waist and flared gently over her hips. The dress's bodice was overlaid with delicate lace, as were the three-quarter-length sleeves. Her hair was swept up in a simple chignon with a few long tendrils framing her face and her only jewellery was a pair of plain gold studs in her ears and the gold chain with the four-leaf clover pendant that had been her father's last gift to her. She looked stunningly beautiful and Torre was aware that Franco stood straighter when Orla walked across the room to join them.

'Orla is my temporary assistant to replace Renzo while he is recovering from his accident,' he explained to the COO after he had made introductions.

'I must say that you are much prettier than Renzo,' Franco murmured as he shook Orla's hand. 'Your name is very beautiful, Orla.'

'Thank you. It's Irish in origin.' She smiled at Franco, who gave her a rather stunned smile in return. Torre felt an unreasonable urge to rearrange his executive's good-looking features with his fist. His phone rang and he strode into a smaller sitting room in the vast suite to take the call from his operations manager in the Philippines.

When he returned to the main lounge five minutes later he found Orla and Franco sitting on the sofa, chatting. Orla's lovely face was animated and the sound of her soft laughter irked Torre even more when he realised that she had never laughed with him, which then begged the question, why did he give a damn?

'It's ten to eight, and you had better get down to the ballroom,' he told Franco curtly. 'Orla and I will follow you shortly.'

Franco departed via the suite's private elevator and Torre walked over to the bar and poured whisky into a glass. He took a long sip of his drink and watched Orla gather up her evening purse and shawl. 'He's married,' he said grimly, before taking another sip of whisky. The single malt felt warm at the back of his throat and sent fire down to his belly. 'I doubt it matters to you that Franco has a wife, but he has a couple of young children, too.'

'Yes, he showed me some photos on his phone of his twin girls. They're little sweethearts.' She frowned. 'Am I missing something here? Why are you at pains to tell me that he's married?'

'In case you had any ideas,' he drawled.

She stared at him. 'What sort of ideas?'

'Oh, come on. Drop the innocent act. You have deliberately worn a dress that will capture the attention of every man at the party. Franco's eyes were practically falling out of their sockets. I'm merely warning you to leave him alone and turn your sorcery on some other poor fool who will be so bewitched by you that he won't realise until it's too late that your pretty smile hides your gold-digger tendencies.'

As he uttered the words, Torre realised that he did not believe them and his accusations were unfounded. He walked over to Orla and guilt stabbed him when he saw her mouth tremble before she quickly firmed her lips. The urge to be close to her consumed and infuriated him.

Lovely though she was, he had known other beautiful women, but none had ever threatened his self-control the way Orla did. He did not understand why she had such a hold over him. The knowledge that he was enslaved by his desire for her, just like his father had been enslaved by her trollop of a mother, filled him with self-contempt.

'My dress is perfectly respectable,' she snapped. 'I am sensitive to Dubai's culture and chose a dress that is not too revealing or risqué. And by the way I paid for it with my own money. I don't expect you or any man to pay for my clothes.' The green flecks in her hazel eyes flashed with fury. 'The truth is I can't do anything right in your opinion, can I, Torre? I could have covered myself from head to toe in sackcloth and you would still accuse me of trying to attract attention.'

She was breathing hard, her cheeks flushed with anger, but he heard the hurt in her voice and he felt an odd sensation as if a hand had squeezed his heart. 'I suppose I'm wearing too much make-up and look like a slut,' she choked, lifting her hand to her brow. 'You have already made the vile suggestion that I was flirting with your work colleague whose name I've forgotten.'

'Franco,' he reminded her. His eyes narrowed. 'Why do you always touch the scar on your head when we argue? How were you injured, incidentally? The scar is only noticeable when I am standing as close to you as I am now, but it must have been a deep wound.'

Orla had stiffened at his mention of the scar above her eyebrow and her tension was almost tangible. 'I've told you I won't discuss my marriage.'

'I didn't ask you about your marriage,' he said mildly, deliberately playing down his curiosity as a shocking suspicion slid into his mind. Something cold and hard settled in the pit of his stomach. A haunted expression had crossed Orla's face at the mention of her marriage, and she looked heartbreakingly fragile. The idea that her famously charming ex-husband could have somehow been responsible for the three-inch scar that ran from the edge of her eyebrow out to her hairline was frankly hard to believe. But the flash of fear in her eyes had been real and had stirred Torre's protective instincts.

'We should go, or we'll be late for the party,' she

said flatly. Her outburst of temper had died and her eyes were dull. Torre wanted to ask her more about her marriage to David Keegan, and with a sense of shock he realised that he did not give a damn about the party to celebrate the company's and his own professional triumph.

He would much rather call room service and have a private dinner served to them in the opulent hotel suite. And he would like to talk to Orla. It was troubling, to say the least, to discover that he wanted more from a woman than merely sex. He wanted more from *this* woman, he amended. He could not recall ever having a meaningful conversation with any of his mistresses. Oh, he'd made small talk as a preliminary to taking them to bed. But none of his previous lovers had fascinated him the way Orla did, so that even the idea of making love to her in the suite's master bedroom where there was a huge mirror on the ceiling above the bed was not his main priority.

Torre shook his head, at a loss to understand what was happening to him. He followed Orla into the elevator and his jaw clenched when she moved as far away as possible from him in the confined space. She eyed him warily and touched the gold-plated chain around her neck, turning the pendant that was supposedly a good luck charm between her fingers.

'I read through the notes you gave me listing the names of the potential new clients who will be at the party,' she said, still in that flat tone, as if she was keeping her emotions under tight control. 'I don't know what you expect me to do as your assistant. If I speak to anyone who happens to be male, I stand to be accused by you of trying to seduce them.' A bitter note crept into

her voice. 'Perhaps you want me to walk two steps behind you and keep my eyes fixed on the floor so that I
don't attract attention.'

'What I would like you to do if at all possible is
try and forget that I behaved like a jerk,' he muttered.
'You look beautiful, and your dress is perfect for the
occasion.'

Her eyes flew to his face. 'I don't understand.'

Torre found himself wishing that he could dismiss
the shadows from her eyes, and guilt knotted in his gut
as he acknowledged that he was responsible for them.
'I'm trying to apologise,' he said roughly. Orla looked
so shocked that he almost laughed. Almost.

CHAPTER EIGHT

THE PARTY WAS a lavish event held in Qasr Jameel's sumptuous ballroom. Designed in the style of an Arabian palace, the vast space was a sea of pink marble, gleaming gold leaf and an exquisite mosaic-tiled floor. Women wearing extravagant evening gowns and men in dinner suits mingled with sheikhs in traditional robes and *keffiyeh*. White-jacketed waiters threaded through the groups of guests to serve champagne cocktails, soft drinks and exquisite canapés that looked far too pretty to eat.

During her brief marriage to David, Orla had accompanied him to a few high-class social functions. His father was a peer and the family seat in Gloucestershire was an imposing mansion where Lady Keegan hosted elegant soirées. Orla had felt out of place at those events and her confidence had been further undermined by David's constant criticism of her. He had invariably found fault with her clothes, and if she dared to wear make-up he'd told her she looked like a tart.

Her dress, which she'd bought from a boutique in Qasr Jameel's shopping complex was elegant without being showy. The last thing she hoped to do was draw attention to herself, which had been Torre's accusation.

She glanced at him standing nearby. Dressed in a black tuxedo and white silk shirt, he was simply devastating. His head was turned slightly away from her while he chatted to another guest and Orla was able to study his chiselled profile.

Predictably her heart skipped a beat. She was growing used to the effect he had on her and she had no control over the molten heat that swept through her veins as she remembered how the stubble on his chin had felt rough against her lips when she'd pressed kisses along his jaw on her way to his mouth. She had been shocked by her wanton behaviour last night. And she'd been even more stunned before the party this evening when Torre had apologised for the horrible things he'd said to her. She could not figure him out and that bothered her. *He* bothered her. She wanted to hate him and the fact that she didn't showed just what a fool she was, she thought bleakly.

Perhaps he sensed her gaze on him for he turned his head towards her and she quickly looked away, but not before she'd seen a gleam in his eyes of amusement and something harder to define that made her feel as though a light had been switched on inside her.

'Orla, I would like you to meet Sheikh Bin al Rashid,' Torre said. 'Orla is my secretarial assistant,' he told the man wearing flowing robes, who was standing beside him.

'I'm pleased to meet you,' Orla murmured as she shook hands with the Sheikh. 'I understand that you are planning to build a similar structure to Qasr Jameel in Bahrain.'

'Indeed. I believe a landmark building such as the one that ARC have delivered here in Dubai would be a draw for businesses and tourists to my country. But I can foresee a problem with the proposed development. The site where I hope the new tower will be constructed is a relatively small area of land in the centre of a busy city and surrounded by other buildings. The construction programme would need to be completed in a short time frame to minimise disruption.'

Orla nodded. 'It was a similar situation here in Dubai. Qasr Jameel stands between other buildings and it was important that the tower be constructed as quickly but also as safely as possible. The civil engineers at ARC used a method of construction called "top down", which allowed the first thirty storeys of the concrete core of the tower to be built before excavation of the basement had been completed. In that way the construction programme and therefore the cost was significantly reduced.'

Warming to her theme, she continued, 'The core of the tower was constructed using a technique known as "slip forming"—where concrete is poured into a continuously moving mould called a formwork, which slides up the building.'

She heard Torre make a muffled sound and realised that she had become carried away with her explanation. On the flight to Dubai early that morning he had given her material to read about ARC's mission statement and business strategies. There had also been a file containing detailed engineering notes about how Qasr Jameel had been constructed.

'There is no need for you to read that particular file. I don't suppose you will find civil engineering processes interesting,' Torre had told her.

In fact, Orla had been fascinated and she'd spent

most of the flight absorbed in studying technical papers. She was surprised and pleased by how much she remembered from when she had been studying for her degree. But she had not finished her qualifications and Torre was one of the leading structural engineers in the world.

'I'm sure you can explain the construction process of Qasr Jameel much better than I can,' she said to him in an embarrassed voice.

His expression was unreadable. 'Your explanation was excellent. I am sure that Sheikh Bin al Rashid would like to hear more—as would I,' he murmured.

'Oh.' She stared at him, wondering if he was making fun of her.

'I am curious to know how it is possible to control the sway of very tall buildings in strong wind,' the Sheikh said.

'That is certainly an important element of the structural design. All tall buildings will move in strong gusts of wind, but it is vital that the occupiers of the building are not affected. Methods to combat the sway effect are by damping the oscillations and also stiffening the central core.' Orla's enthusiasm for the subject replaced her diffidence and she spent several minutes expounding on the building methods used in the construction of skyscrapers.

When she had finished, Sheikh Rashid turned to Torre. 'I confess I am surprised and impressed that your secretarial assistant has such an in-depth knowledge of building processes.'

'Yes, Orla is full of surprises,' Torre replied drily. His thoughtful gaze rested on her face. Fortunately, at that moment a prince from Dubai's royal family stepped onto the dais at one end of the ballroom and made a speech before declaring Qasr Jameel officially open. Orla hoped to use the distraction to slip away from Torre and lose herself in the throng of guests, but he put his hand on her arm and instructed her to stay next to him.

'I may need you,' he drawled when she looked mulish. He did not specify in what way he might need her and she thought it wiser not to ask when she saw a predatory gleam in his eyes that made her heart thump.

More speeches and a media conference followed. In the press room, photographers wanted pictures of Torre and the team of ARC engineers who had worked on the Qasr Jameel tower. 'I am only your temporary assistant, and there's no need for me to be in the photos,' Orla pointed out when Torre ordered her to stand beside him while camera flashes went off. But somehow she found herself crushed close to his side in the group photo.

Worse was to come when he led her onto the dance floor and drew her into his arms. Through her dress she could feel the muscles and sinews of his powerful thighs pressed up against her, and the hard ridge of his arousal pressing into the cradle of her pelvis brought a betraying stain of colour to her cheeks. There was a brief lull in the music before the next tune started and she gave a yawn that was not entirely fake.

It was only two days ago since she had left London for Amalfi, feeling apprehensive at the prospect of meeting Torre again. With good reason, as it had turned out. Her friendship with Jules had changed for ever, and she had made a pact with the devil when she had signed a contract that gave Torre control over her life for the next two months.

'I'm afraid you will have to manage without me for the rest of the party.' She yawned again. 'I think jet-lag must be catching up with me. I'm sure you won't be lonely for long. The blonde in the almost-see-through dress who you were flirting with earlier has been sending me evil stares while we've been dancing,' she added waspishly.

Torre grinned and tightened his arm around her waist when she attempted to move away from him. 'The green flecks in your eyes are more noticeable when you are jealous, *gattina mia*,' he murmured.

'I'm not *jealous*. And I'm not your kitten.'

His eyes gleamed like molten silver. 'I have your claw marks on my back to prove it.'

She felt warmth spread over her face and an even fierier heat swept through her and settled right there between her legs where last night he had caressed her with his clever fingers, arousing her to a fever pitch of desire. When he'd moved over her and possessed her with his hard, thrusting body she remembered that she had raked her nails down his shoulders in the ecstasy of her mind-blowing orgasm.

She did not dare look at Torre as he steered her across the ballroom and into an elevator that whisked them up to the Presidential Suite. As soon as she was inside the suite, Orla kicked off her high-heeled shoes and gave a sigh of relief as she curled her toes into the thick carpet. She intended to go straight to her bedroom, which was on the other side of the main lounge from the master bedroom, but Torre's voice made her halt halfway across the room.

'I find it hard to believe that you gained in-depth knowledge of the complex structural engineering challenges involved in the construction of super-tall towers when you worked as a secretary at a small building company,' he said as he walked over to the bar. 'Would you like a drink?' When she shook her head, he continued. 'I checked, and Mayall's main line of business is coastal defence projects, not skyscrapers.' He poured himself a glass of whisky and took a long sip before he strolled over to where she was edging past the sofa, hoping to escape down the hallway that led to her bedroom.

'I am intrigued by you, Orla,' he murmured. He lifted his hand and brushed a few loose tendrils of hair back from her face. She stiffened when his fingers brushed very lightly over her scar. 'Just when I think I know who you are, you surprise me.'

'You don't know me at all.' She did not understand why it made her feel so sad. Sometimes she wondered if anyone had ever really known her, or had even bothered to try. Certainly not her mother, or the man she had spent ten hellish months married to. 'And what you think you know about me is wrong,' she told Torre.

'So enlighten me,' he invited softly. 'Explain to me how I might have misjudged you?'

'I *didn't* have an ulterior motive when I made love with you eight years ago.' She struggled to swallow past the sudden constriction in her throat. 'I know what my mother was,' she said flatly. 'She married your father for his money and I understand why you despised her. But when I lost my virginity to you I thought...' She shook her head, the lump of misery inside her seeming to expand and fill her lungs so that she found it hard to breathe. 'I was young with a head full of romantic dreams. Back then I still believed that princes existed.'

She glanced up at him and noticed an odd expression in his eyes that made her heart thump.

'Where did you go that morning? I followed you downstairs a few minutes after you ran out of my room but you had disappeared.'

'Did you think I would stick around after you'd called me a gold-digger? I caught a bus back to Villa Romano. My mother's friends had arranged for a taxi to take them to the airport, and I left with them.'

Torre let out a heavy sigh. 'My father had mentioned that you worked in a bar in London. Did you go back to your job?'

'It was only a part-time job so that I could earn some money when I started university.' Orla felt a little spurt of satisfaction when he looked surprised.

'I didn't know that you had a degree. It's not on your CV. What subject is it in?'

'I studied civil engineering for three and a half years.'

He stared at her—she guessed it was probably the first time that Torre Romano had been rendered speechless—and then gave a low laugh. 'That explains how you were able to do such a good job when you spoke to Sheikh Bin al Rashid. Thanks to you, he is so impressed by the quality of staff that work for ARC that the company is a serious contender to win the commission to build a skyscraper in Bahrain. But I don't understand why you did not apply for a civil engineering job at ARC, or why you worked in a secretarial role at Mayall's.'

'I left university without graduating,' she muttered.

'Why?' He frowned when she did not reply. 'Many students become stressed about sitting exams. Is that why you left? I remember feeling under pressure when I was writing a thesis for my research doctorate in structural design.'

'No, it wasn't exam pressure. I dropped out of university when I got married.' She bit her lip, remembering how David had taken control of her life.

Torre's expression hardened. 'You thought you would not need qualifications or a career because your wealthy husband would keep you?'

'*No*, it wasn't that. I deeply regret that I didn't graduate. David persuaded me to postpone finishing my degree because he travelled abroad a lot to play cricket and he wanted me with him. I always intended to go back to university but after my marriage ended I desperately needed to earn money. My mother was ill—' She broke off abruptly, aware that bringing Kimberly into the conversation would not win her any sympathy from Torre.

'Despite what you might have read in the tabloids, I did not receive any kind of maintenance pay-out from David. I had to wait for two years before he agreed to a divorce and I wanted nothing from him apart from my freedom.' Her voice shook. 'I learned that to be free to live my life on my terms was—*is*—more valuable than anything.'

Torre did not know how to deal with the riot of his emotions. Ever since he had been told by a nanny when he was six years old that he must not cry at his mother's funeral because he might upset his father, he had kept his feelings locked deep inside him. Life was much easier without the highs and lows of riding an emotional roller-coaster and allowed him to focus on his career.

He enjoyed engineering because it required him to use the analytical side of his brain to solve complex problems. The rules of maths and physics were far easier to understand than unstructured, messy emotions that too often ignored common sense.

Only once since he was a young boy had he listened to his heart rather than his head. He'd been kicking his heels, bored out of his skull at that damned party following his father's ill-conceived wedding to a woman who had made a career out of marrying and divorcing rich men.

Torre had been about to leave; full of self-righteous satisfaction that he would never be led by his libido like Giuseppe. He'd been halfway out of the door when something had made him turn his head and he'd looked across the room. As he'd stared at Orla his only thought had been that he had to have her, had to possess her impossible beauty, her creamy skin and pale red hair, those eyes that turned from hazel to green when she was aroused and her mouth that promised myriad sensual delights.

His tight grip on his self-control had unravelled and been replaced with an urgent need he had never felt for any other woman. That was what had appalled him most the next morning when he'd discovered Orla's identity. Like mother, like daughter, a voice in his head had mocked him, and he'd been unable to think of one reason why Orla would have given her virginity to him— other than because she'd thought he would pay for the privilege by putting a ring on her finger.

Now, as he watched her expression become wary, he acknowledged that he had directed his anger with himself onto Orla rather than have to admit that he'd

failed to live up to his high ideals. And he'd been horrified by the idea that he needed her. *Need* suggested a
lack of control, but without iron self-control he would
have wept at his *mamma*'s funeral instead of blinking
back his tears.

Torre pictured himself at six years old. He had been
very brave, his father had praised him afterwards when
they had returned to the house and left his *mamma* alone
in the graveyard where she had been buried. It had been
hard not to cry when he'd thought of her lying in a box
beneath the earth, but he'd wanted to please his father
and so he had dug his fingernails into the palms of his
hands until they'd made little crescents on his skin to
remind himself that brave boys didn't cry.

He forced his mind away from the painful memories
of his childhood. His thoughts turned to the morning
after the first time he'd slept with Orla, when she had
woken in his bed at the old farmhouse in Ravello. He
had watched her golden eyelashes sweep upwards and
a soft pink stain had spread over her face when she'd
stared at him lying beside her. He'd touched her breasts
and seen her eyes change from hazel to olive-green as
she'd felt his excitement. Desire had run hot and urgent
through his veins. But it had been more than that. He'd
experienced a sense of completeness that he'd never felt
with any other woman and he'd known that one night
with her had not been enough. He'd wanted more, he'd
wanted her—

For ever. The thought had slipped into his mind and
refused to budge.

The strident ring of her phone had been an unwelcome intrusion and he'd struggled to hide his frustration when she'd sat up and reached for her handbag on

the bedside table. 'It's probably Kimberly. I'll have to take the call,' Orla told him. He'd remembered then that she'd said she was one of his new stepmother's retinue of assistants.

In her haste to find her phone, Orla had tipped the contents of her bag onto the bed. Torre remembered his incomprehension when he'd seen his mother's emerald earrings sparkling on the sheet.

'Why were these in your bag?'

She'd looked at the earrings and shrugged. 'I was worried I would lose them at the party so I put them in my bag.'

'But how did you come to have them in your possession?'

She seemed puzzled by his curt tone. 'My mother lent them to me. Giuseppe gave Kimberly several pieces of jewellery as wedding presents, and she said I could borrow the earrings to wear with the dress that I borrowed from her.'

'Kimberly Connaught is your *mother*?' A lead weight had dropped into the pit of his stomach. The sickening realisation that he was as much of a fool as his father had evoked bitter shame in his heart. 'Why didn't you tell me?' He'd laughed hollowly at himself. 'Stupid question.'

'I didn't think you would be interested...' She'd flushed. 'We didn't talk much last night.'

No, he had been too obsessed with taking her to bed, Torre had acknowledged. He'd vented his anger with himself by accusing Orla of deliberately deceiving him.

Back then I still believed that princes existed. The comment she'd made a few minutes ago filled him with shame. *Dio,* far from acting like a chivalrous prince, he had vilified her so that she had fled from his home in Ravello on a goddamned bus. For eight years she had avoided seeing him again, even arranging to visit her mother at Villa Romano only when she'd known he would not be there.

Had he been wrong about her? he brooded. 'Your marriage lasted for less than a year. Why did you marry a wealthy sportsman who also happens to be the sole heir to his family's large fortune, if not for his money?'

'I thought I loved David. He can be very charming and... I was lonely.' There was a faint tremor in her voice. 'He seemed kind.'

Torre frowned as he watched her mouth tremble and he sensed the effort it cost her to firm her lips. '*Was* he kind?'

'No,' she whispered, almost as if she was ashamed. But why would she be ashamed of her ex-husband's failings? Anger ran swift and hot through Torre—not with Orla, or even with himself in this instance, but with her ex-husband. He was hardly in a position to judge, he acknowledged, when his own treatment of Orla was not something he was proud of. But when she had spoken of David Keegan there had been fear in her eyes.

'Orla...' He caught hold of her arms as she went to step past him. She stiffened but made no attempt to pull away from him when he turned her to face him. 'You know I would never harm you,' he said softly. It was important to him that she knew she could trust him.

She stared at him for a moment and then nodded her head. 'I believe you. But right now I'm tired and I want to go to bed—alone.' Delicate colour winged along her high cheekbones when he smiled.

'If that's really what you want then of course you

are free to go to your own bed,' he murmured, releasing her arm. 'The first time we met, the chemistry between us was white hot,' he reminded her, 'and *eight years* later it is just as explosive. Do you think we can simply ignore it?'

'I am your temporary assistant, and that's all I want to be,' she whispered. But she still did not move away from him and he noticed the pulse at the base of her throat jumped erratically.

'Your eyes turn green when you lie.' He lifted his hand and trailed his fingers down the front of her dress, between the high, firm mounds of her breasts. It was the lightest touch, but she flushed and he heard her breath catch in her throat. He understood, because he too felt the wild heat, the uncontrollable longing that defied reason or logic. 'You want to be under me, don't you, *cara*? You ache for me as much as I ache to make love to you.'

Her eyes gleamed with green fire. 'Yes, *damn you,*' she said fiercely. 'You are like a drug in my veins and I can't think straight when I'm near you.'

With a groan Torre pulled her into his arms and he was amazed by how perfectly her slender curves fitted against his big, hard body like two pieces of a jigsaw. He sought her mouth and his heart kicked in his chest when she parted her lips. She gave a soft sigh of capitulation and melted into him as if she realised the futility of trying to hold back the tidal wave that crashed over both of them and sucked them down into a maelstrom of desire.

Without taking his mouth from hers, he lifted her into his arms and carried her into the master bedroom, which had been styled like a sultan's harem with black silk sheets on the bed and that huge mirror on the ceiling. He set her on her feet and reached behind her to slide the zip of her dress down the length of her spine. Slowly he drew the confection of silk and lace from her body until she stood there in her pretty underwear; a sheer black bra through which the rosy crests of her nipples were visible, and a pair of tiny, black lace panties.

He rocked back on his heels and simply looked at her, taking his fill of her fine-boned beauty and anticipating when she would be completely naked and writhing beneath him. Maybe he would lie on his back and lift her on top of him so that he could watch them in the mirror above the bed. The erotic images in his mind sent a surge of heat down to his groin.

Finally Torre admitted to himself that he had compared every lover he'd had in the past eight years to Orla. No other woman had made him *shake* with desire like she did. The voice of his sanity was all but drowned out by the thunder of his heart, but still it whispered a warning that she was dangerous. She was a sorceress and it would be too easy to fall under her spell. But he assured himself that once he'd possessed her again, once he'd assuaged the ravenous beast inside him, his obsession with her would surely start to fade and he would regain control of a situation that frankly he had never imagined he would find himself in—a slave to his desire for a woman who had the face of an angel and a sexy body that promised untold sensual delights.

He stripped with swift efficiency, dropping his shirt onto the floor and removing his shoes and socks before stepping out of his trousers. Another time he would enjoy having her undress him, but not now when he was desperate to be inside her. *Desperate* went against everything he'd thought he was, everything he wanted to be. But he had stopped kidding himself that he had any control over his response to Orla.

Her eyes widened when he pulled off his boxers and his erection sprang, thick and long and so very hard from the mass of black hairs growing at its base. He could see the hard points of her nipples outlined beneath her bra and he longed to taste them. With a grunt of impatience he reached behind her again to unfasten her bra and when it fell to the floor he captured her breasts in his hands, spreading his fingers possessively over the pale globes with their dusky pink tips tilted provocatively towards him, as if begging for him to take them into his mouth.

He resisted the temptation while he hooked his fingers into the top of her panties and tugged them down her legs. And then he lifted her and laid her down on the bed, and he had never seen anything more beautiful than Orla's slender, milky-pale body stretched out on the black silk sheets, her rose-gold hair spread across the pillows and the green flecks in her eyes casting her magic on him. It was all he could do not to take her there and then, to simply push her legs apart and thrust into her molten heat. The sweet scent of her arousal heightened his urgent need, but when he lifted himself over her and saw a flicker of uncertainty in her eyes he silently cursed his crass impatience.

She had intimated that her marriage had been an unhappy experience and her ex-husband had not been kind. Torre did not know what to make of the implications of that, or why she refused to explain the scar that ran from above her eyebrow out to her hairline. His suspicion that David Keegan might have been responsible filled him with cold fury.

He wanted her more than he had ever wanted any woman, but right now she looked unbearably fragile, and he needed her with him, a willing partner, not a sacrificial lamb. His chest expanded as he took a deep breath. He shifted his position so that he was kneeling above her, and leaned forward to kiss her mouth, coaxing her lips apart with his tongue so that he could explore her inner sweetness.

Slowly she relaxed and he heard her give a shaky sigh as she curled her arms around his neck. He liked it when she ran her fingers through his hair and the inherent tenderness in the way she stroked his face tugged on something buried deep inside him. His hunger for her still burned fiercely; but *this* was something else and he did not want the kiss to end. Instead it became ever more erotic and by the time he lifted his head and dragged air into his lungs he was shaking with an intensity of desire that was beyond anything he had ever felt before.

But he still made himself wait. It struck him that the two previous times he'd made love to Orla it had been on his terms. With a stab of guilt he acknowledged that his need for her had made him impatient. But now he took his time as he trailed his lips over her throat and across the slopes of her breasts, tasting her creamy skin and revelling in its satiny softness. Her nipples puckered as his warm breath grazed them, and when he drew one hard nub into his mouth and sucked, she made a choked sound that caused the beast inside him to roar.

She was his. The thought pushed into his mind and he should have been horrified by the possessiveness that surged through him. Instead it felt…right.

He skimmed his hand over her flat stomach and continued down to the V of neatly trimmed red-gold curls between her thighs. A tremor ran through her when he eased her legs apart and rubbed a finger over her, finding her slick heat as he gently parted her. She caught her breath as he slid one finger inside her, then two, while simultaneously he applied pressure with his thumb to her sensitised flesh.

'Oh.' She shuddered and jerked her hips towards his hand, her fingers clutching the silk sheets. A rosy flush of sexual heat spread over her face and breasts, and he felt the ripples of her orgasm squeeze and release his fingers. But Torre wasn't done with her yet, not nearly. She gave a soft moan of protest when he withdrew his fingers and then stiffened as he nudged her legs wider open with his shoulders and lowered his mouth to her feminine heat. 'You can't...' she whispered, sounding appalled yet excited, her fingernails digging into his back as she held onto him.

'Hold on tight, *gattina mia*,' he told her thickly, and then he bent his head and breathed in the sweet scent of her sex as he used his tongue with devastating effect.

She came apart utterly, and he delighted in the sound of her ragged breaths and the husky moans she made as he pleasured her with his mouth. He tasted the nectar of her femininity and groaned when she raked her nails down his back and buttocks. Her wild response evoked a primitive hunger in him that would not, *could* not be controlled.

'Now, Torre...*please.*'

With a low growl he positioned himself over her and hooked her legs over his shoulders. And then he claimed her, thrusting into her eager body with deep, measured strokes that tested his self-control to its limits. She felt like velvet surrounding the rigid steel of his body. Soft against hard, her slender body so pale against his darkly tanned skin.

He would never have enough of her. The words sang in his heart as his body soared higher and he drove them both on, on, until she suddenly gasped and sobbed his name as her body convulsed around him.

At last he reaped the rewards for his patience. His control splintered as he surged into her one more time. Buried deep in her wild heat he came so hard that he felt ripped apart by the force of his climax.

For a long time afterwards he simply lay on top of her, his body lax and his face against her throat as his heart rate gradually returned to its normal, steady beat. He was reluctant to move, but he was aware that his weight must be heavy on her and shifted to lie next to her, propping himself up on one elbow.

'Well, *gattina*,' he murmured, but Orla silenced him by holding her fingers across his mouth.

'Don't.'

He frowned and she said huskily, 'This is the point when you are no doubt going to say something horrible, and I... I can't deal with it tonight.'

Her words felt like a punch in his gut, made worse because he knew he deserved her wariness. 'I was going to say that you are perfect.' His mouth curved into a wry smile. 'And you are without doubt the most beautiful engineer I have ever met.'

Again her bottom lip gave a little quiver that made him want to cover her mouth with his and kiss her better. 'I'm not an engineer,' she said flatly. 'I told you I didn't finish my BSc in civil engineering.'

'Why don't you go back to studying and sit your

final exams? It was clear from hearing you talking to Sheikh Bin al Rashid that you have a good knowledge of engineering principles.'

'I can't afford the university fees. Anyway, there's a good chance I'd fail the exams.' She gave a heavy sigh. 'David didn't believe that I was clever enough to have a career in engineering.'

'On what grounds did he make that assumption?' Torre managed to disguise the blast of red-hot anger he felt towards a man he had never met.

Orla did not answer him and when he looked at her, he saw that she had fallen asleep. Her hand was tucked under her cheek and her long, golden eyelashes lay on her pale skin. She was as fragile—and as prickly—as an English rose, he thought, and once again he felt an odd tug in his chest. Tonight in his arms she had revealed a bewitching sensuality that had blown his mind.

He was already hard again and he was tempted to wake her and enjoy her delectable body for a second time, take them both on a ride that would end with their mutual satisfaction of an explosive orgasm. Every time he made love to her would, he was confident, take him closer to the point of satiation and his fascination with her, this damnable desire that roared like a ravenous beast inside him, would simply wither and die.

But it was likely that she was suffering from jet-lag after the long-haul flight to Dubai. She was sleeping peacefully and he did not have the heart to disturb her. As he strode into the en suite bathroom and stood beneath the shower, Torre reminded himself that his *heart* was in no way involved with Orla.

CHAPTER NINE

TEN DAYS LATER, Orla followed Torre down the steps of the ARC private jet after it had landed at London City Airport. Drizzle was falling from a leaden sky and the temperature was at least ten degrees lower than it had been in Dubai and cooler than in Rome, where they had attended a party at ARC's headquarters to mark the company's centenary. Both the official opening of Qasr Jameel in Dubai and ARC's one hundred years celebrations had attracted international media interest.

Walking through the airport's arrivals lounge, Orla was horrified when she saw pictures of her and Torre on the front pages of several newspapers. The caption above a photo of them dancing together at the party read: *Italy's sexiest CEO and his stunning assistant— the construction industry's most glamorous couple?*

'I bet you wouldn't have danced with your usual assistant,' she muttered.

Torre looked amused. 'To be fair, you are a lot prettier than Renzo.' They exited the concourse and he led her towards a black limousine, nodding to the chauffeur who opened the rear door for them to climb into the car.

'It's not funny,' Orla insisted as she secured her seatbelt and the car moved off. 'I like my job, even though it is only temporary. I don't want the other staff at ARC to guess that I'm sleeping with you.'

He gave a careless shrug. 'It does not matter what anyone else thinks.'

'It does to me.' She bit her lip. 'I've seen on the company's internal website that another secretarial position will become vacant at ARC UK in a couple of months' time, and the recruiting process is starting now. I'd like to apply for the job, but if I am offered it I want it to be on my own merits and not because everyone knows that I'm in a relationship with the chairman of the company.'

'Relationship?' Torre's cool voice sent a chill through Orla. 'I don't know what you think is happening, *cara*, but it certainly is not a relationship.'

'What is it then?' she demanded, hiding her sense of hurt with anger. 'We have spent every one of the last ten days working together and we've shared a bed every night.' They had shared a lot more than just a bed, she thought ruefully. Their passion had grown more intense every night as they had discovered the secrets of each other's bodies and learned how to give one another the utmost pleasure.

She was aware of Torre's surprise at her outburst of temper, and in truth she had shocked herself. Her marriage to David had taught her to suppress her emotions but Torre's scathing tone made her see red.

How dared he speak to her in that dismissive way? she thought furiously. He wasn't always so controlled. She knew how to use her hands and lips on him to make him groan. Only this morning, when they had shared the shower cubicle at his exquisite apartment in Rome, she had knelt in front of him and pleasured him with her mouth while he'd threaded his fingers into her hair and muttered that she was a sorceress.

'We have sex,' he said harshly, as if he'd read her mind. 'Very good sex, admittedly, but that's all it is. In a little over six weeks Renzo will return to his job as my assistant, and I fully expect that the inconvenient sexual attraction between you and I will have burned out.' His grey eyes were as hard as steel. 'I don't have relationships.'

'Why is that?' She ignored his frown warning her that he wanted her to drop the subject. On some level she realised that she was deliberately provoking him, which she would never have risked doing with David. 'I wonder if your fear of forming meaningful relationships stems from losing your mother when you were young,' she mused aloud. 'You said you were six when she died. I was ten when I lost my father. It's such a shock and nothing prepares you for how much it hurts *here*.' She pressed her hand over her heart.

Beside her, Torre stiffened and the furious gleam in his eyes told her to back off. So why didn't she do the sensible thing? Orla wondered. Maybe it was because she sensed that she had touched a raw nerve in him. 'Who took care of you after your mum died? Giuseppe must have been busy running ARC, but did he encourage you to talk about your mother and grieve for her?'

He swore savagely. 'What the hell is this? If you must know, I was looked after by nannies until Giuseppe married my stepmother Sandrine. I never spoke about my mother's death to anyone. I understood that my father found it upsetting and so I did not mention her and neither did he.' He slashed his hand through the air. 'I'm really not interested in your amateur psychoanalysis.'

She looked at him and saw beneath his scowl the heartbroken boy he must have been when he had lost his mother. 'You said you don't have relationships, but you were engaged once,' she reminded him. 'Jules said that your fiancée decided not to marry you. But he thought you were still in love with Marisa.'

Torre's brows rose. The brief flash of vulnerability Orla thought she'd seen on his face had disappeared and his sculpted features were as coldly beautiful as marble. 'Jules knows nothing about my private life,' he said icily. 'And while we are on the subject of my stepbrother—if you were hoping to get a job at ARC UK so that you can see Jules, forget it. He has moved to Tokyo to take charge of the accounts department at the Japanese branch of ARC.'

'My decision to apply for a job at the London office has nothing to do with Jules.' Orla felt a pang of guilt that she had hardly given Jules a thought since he had left Villa Romano after she'd turned down his marriage proposal. Her every waking thought and even her dreams when she'd fallen into an exhausted sleep after making love with Torre for hours had been dominated by him.

While they had been in Dubai they'd visited two other ARC construction projects, and before going to Rome they had stopped in Serbia to inspect the final phase of a shopping mall development that ARC was set to complete on schedule. Orla had accompanied Torre on site visits to the projects and she'd been fascinated by all aspects of the construction process.

'I've just received a message from the project manager of the Harbour Side development, asking if we can meet him at ten o'clock tomorrow morning,' Torre told

her, glancing up from his phone. 'I'm interested to see
the site now that demolition of the old printing works
that stood there is nearly complete.'

Orla knew that Harbour Side was an exciting new
project for ARC UK, with plans to create a residential
area with houses, a school, community centre, shops
and leisure facilities in a run-down area of London's
Docklands. It was exactly the kind of project she would
have loved to be part of if she had qualified as a civil
engineer. Once again she felt a sharp pang of regret
that she had not finished her engineering degree. It was
hard to accept that she had allowed David to have so
much power over her when he had put pressure on her
to drop out of university.

Wasn't she making the same mistake with Torre? The
thought sent shockwaves through her. She did not fear
that he would abuse her like her ex-husband had done.
He was a generous and unexpectedly tender lover. The
problem was her, Orla acknowledged heavily. Torre
had made it clear that he regarded their relationship as
temporary, but she knew she was halfway to falling in
love with him.

She stared out of the window as the car crawled along
in the London traffic. They were on their way to an exclusive hotel in Mayfair, where Torre had asked her to
book them a suite for two nights before they were due
to return to Italy. Her treacherous body was impatient
for him to make love to her and take her to the magical
place of tumultuous passion that was uniquely theirs.
But afterwards would come the self-recrimination because she knew that Torre was only using her body for
sexual gratification. She did not think she could bear

it tonight when her emotions felt as though they had been scraped raw.

Her phone rang from the depths of her handbag but by the time she had located it, the ring tone had stopped. She noticed that she had a number of missed calls, but before she had time to see who they were from she received a text from her neighbour Mandy.

Are you free tonight? Do you fancy sharing a bottle of wine and a pizza?

An evening spent chatting to a girlfriend and a night alone in her own bed was exactly what she needed, Orla decided. She turned to Torre. 'While we are in London I'd like to go home to my flat. I need to catch up on a few things and collect any post.' No doubt there would be a stack of bills from her mother's creditors waiting for her.

She was surprised that Torre did not argue and, in fact, she sensed that he was relieved. Perhaps he was tiring of her already? Her heart clenched. She knew he was often in London for work and it was likely that he had another mistress who he could summon to his hotel to entertain him, she thought bleakly.

'Can you ask the driver to drop me at the next underground station? I'll take the tube to Islington.'

He frowned. 'I thought you lived with your mother at the penthouse apartment in Chelsea that Giuseppe gave to Kimberly as part of her divorce settlement?'

'The apartment was sold when my mother went to America.' Orla did not explain that she had used the proceeds from the sale of the flat, after the mortgage had been paid off, to pay some of Kimberley's medical bills.

'Give the driver your address,' Torre told her. 'He can drop you home before driving me to the hotel.'

Twenty minutes later, the limousine drew up outside a tall Victorian house in North London. Orla quickly got out of the car while the chauffeur retrieved her suit-case from the boot. She hoped Torre would not suggest that she invite him in. 'I'll meet you at the Harbour Side development tomorrow morning,' she told him before she hurried up the front path.

From the outside the house looked impressively large, but inside it had been turned into ten studio flats. Orla's flat was in the attic and the sloping ceilings made the cramped living space even smaller. She had done her best to make the flat homely with a rug covering the threadbare carpet and brightly coloured cushions on the bed. The door opened directly into the flat's one main room, which doubled up as a bedroom and sitting room. Through another door was a tiny kitchen area and beyond it a shower room.

She dropped her suitcase and handbag onto the bed and collapsed into the well-worn armchair. It was hard to believe it was only two weeks ago that Jules had collected her from her flat and driven her to the air-port for their flight to Naples. So much had happened since then. *Torre had happened since then.* She felt as though she had been riding a roller-coaster and now suddenly the ride had stopped and she was trying to get her breath back.

As she had predicted, there had been a pile of let-ters in her pigeon hole down in the entrance hall. Be-fore she dealt with them she changed out of her work clothes, swapping her elegant skirt and blouse for faded jeans and a soft grey sweater, and replacing her stiletto heels with comfortable trainers. With a sigh of relief she pulled the pins from her chignon and as her hair unravelled down her back she massaged her scalp with her fingertips.

While she was filling the kettle to make a much-needed cup of tea, there was a knock on the door. Guessing it was Mandy from the flat below, Orla quickly crossed the room and her heart gave a lurch when she opened the door and found herself staring at Torre's broad chest. Would he always have such a devastating impact on her? she wondered despairingly. His tall, muscular frame filled the doorway, but it wasn't just his physical size that was overwhelming—it was his impossibly handsome face, the swathe of almost black hair that he pushed off his brow and his discerning grey eyes that seemed to see into her soul.

'What are you doing here?' Surprise made her voice sharp. She did not want him to see how she lived and she stood in front of him to prevent him from stepping into the flat. But he pushed past her with insulting ease, frowning as he took in the shabby furnishings and peeling paintwork. Orla could have died when his gaze lingered on the clothes drying rack that was festooned with her knickers.

'I'll ask you the same question,' he said tersely. 'Why do you live in this shoebox?'

'Because it's all I can afford. The cost of renting in London is astronomical.'

He gave her a close look. 'You said you did not receive the huge divorce settlement from your ex-husband that was rumoured in the press, but you must have come out of your marriage with some sort of financial security.'

She shook her head. 'I wanted *nothing* from David.'

Torre seemed taken aback by her fierce denial. After a moment he said, 'Couldn't your mother have helped you after you were sacked from Mayall's? God knows, she made a fortune from my father's inability to spot a gold-digger.'

Orla gathered up the opened letters on the bed. One was a bill from the specialist stroke hospital in Chicago where her mother had spent the past few months, and another was from a loan company, demanding repayment of the money she had borrowed to pay some of Kimberley's creditors. When Orla had discovered the extent of her mother's financial problems she had taken responsibility for her debts.

'My mother spent all the money your father gave her,' she said flatly. 'She's hopeless with money and blew most of her divorce settlement on a champagne lifestyle and some ill-advised investments.' Torre gave a snort, and she said quietly, 'I know you despise my mother but Giuseppe is more astute that you give him credit for. I think he knew she was attracted to his wealth but he married her anyway. Kimberly had a terrible childhood. She was raped by an uncle when she was fourteen and she ran away from home and ended up living on the streets.'

She slumped down onto the bed. 'My mother suffered a stroke while she was in America and almost died. I lost my job at Mayall's because I had to take so much time off work to visit her in Chicago. While I sat at her bedside in the hospital she told me what had happened to her when she was young.'

Orla sighed. 'Ironically, just before she became ill, Kimberly fell in love with a really nice man who isn't wealthy. Neville married her in the hospital chapel. She has serious health problems from the stroke but Nev is devoted to her. The specialist is optimistic my mother will regain some of her mobility, but medical treatment in America is expensive. When Jules told me about the vacancy for a PA at ARC UK I was desperate for the job so that I could continue to pay for Kimberly's care.'

Torre sat down next to her on the bed and she heard him expel his breath on a heavy sigh. 'And so when you were turned down for the job at the London office you accepted my offer to work as my temporary assistant.'

'That was one reason.' The words left her lips before she could stop them and she blushed when he gave her an intent look that pierced through the layers of her defences.

'What was the other reason?' His voice was not sardonic, as it so often was, and his steel-grey eyes had softened to the colour of woodsmoke. He was so *big* in her tiny flat. Earlier in the car he had pulled off his tie and undone the top buttons on his shirt, and Orla's gaze was fixated on the expanse of his darkly tanned skin covered with black chest hairs. The evocative fragrance of his aftershave teased her senses, and she knew with a sharp pang of sadness that in a few weeks from now, when she only had his memory to hold onto at night and he had doubtless forgotten her, she would always associate the scent of sandalwood with him.

He lifted his hand to tuck a lock of her hair behind her ear before he brushed his fingertips down her cheek. 'Well, *cara*?'

'You know why,' she whispered. 'I wanted to find out if…' She broke off and moistened her dry lips with the tip of her tongue.

'If the white-hot chemistry between us still burned as fiercely,' he finished for her. He slid his hand beneath her chin and angled his mouth over hers. 'It was for the very reason that I gave you a job that entailed us spending every day and, I hoped, every night together.'

She went up in flames the instant his lips claimed hers. It was always the same, she had zero ability to resist him, but now, instead of hating herself for her weakness, she made the decision to savour every moment she spent in his arms, fully aware that it wouldn't last for ever.

He deepened the kiss, sliding his tongue into her mouth as he tumbled them both down so that they were lying side by side on the bed. She ran her hands over his shirt, feeling the heat of his body through the fine silk and the erratic thud of his heart beneath her palm. Their clothes were a frustrating barrier and she tugged his shirt buttons open while he slid his hand beneath her sweater and gave a husky growl of satisfaction when he discovered she was braless.

Orla moaned as Torre spread his fingers possessively over one breast and teased its hard tip with his thumb, sending exquisite sensations shooting down to the hot, eager place between her legs. The sudden loud peal of the landline phone barely impinged on her consciousness and after a few rings the answering-machine was activated.

'Are you having fun with your lover boy? You filthy bitch.' David's voice was slurred, a sure sign that he had been drinking.

Orla tensed in Torre's arms. She wanted to rush across to the phone and cut the call, but her limbs refused to move and she felt sick as her ex-husband's voice continued.

'He'll soon discover what a waste of space you are. Has he found out yet that the way to keep you in line is with a few slaps?'

The line went dead but David's mocking laughter still echoed in Orla's ears. She did not dare look at Torre, could not bear to see the disgust in his eyes that he must surely feel.

She froze as a phone rang again, not the landline this time but her mobile. She stared uncomprehendingly as Torre pulled her phone out of his jacket pocket. 'You left it in the car. That's why I came up to your flat, to return it to you,' he told her, sounding grim.

Orla took the phone from him just as the ring tone ceased and saw that she had ten missed calls from David. There were also several texts from her ex-husband and it was not necessary for her to read them to know that they would be as poisonous and vitriolic as his phone message a moment ago.

'What the *hell*?' Torre growled. The landline phone rang again and he jumped up, strode across the room and snatched the handset out of its holder. 'If you attempt to contact Orla again you had better pray that the law deals with you before I do, Keegan,' he snarled before he cut the call.

'*Don't*. Oh, my God,' Orla whispered. 'That will just make things worse. He'll be angry now, and when David is angry he's not a nice person.'

She stood up from the bed and automatically lifted her hand to the scar above her eyebrow. Torre walked towards her and she crossed her arms defensively over her chest, creating a physical barrier to keep him from getting too close.

'He *hit* you?' There was something in Torre's voice

that Orla had never heard before. Anger, ruthlessly controlled, but also a note of pity that made her want to
sink through the floor.

'Go away.' She tried to sound forceful but her voice
was thick with tears that clogged her throat. '*Please*
leave. I don't want you here.'

He ignored her and ran his finger lightly over her
scar. 'Keegan did this, didn't he?' His jaw clenched.
'What exactly did he do?'

Torre put his hands on her shoulders to prevent her
from pulling away from him. Even if she could run
away from her humiliation, where would she go? Orla
thought bleakly, and in that moment she had never felt
so alone. The fight drained out of her and her shoulders slumped.

'The verbal abuse started on our honeymoon. Up
until our wedding David had always been charming and
I didn't have an inkling that there was another side to
him, a very nasty side.' She sighed. 'Within weeks of
marrying him I knew I had made a mistake but I had
nowhere to go and no one to talk to. My mother had her
own life, and I didn't want to admit to my friends who
had been envious when I'd married a famous sportsman and celebrity that David was a bully. Whenever we
were out in public he was nice to me. He has a Jekyll
and Hyde personality. Everyone who meets him thinks
he is wonderful,' she said heavily.

'I started to believe that he was right when he said
the problems in our marriage were my fault. I tried my
hardest to please him, but nothing I ever did was right.'
She swallowed. 'I was scared of him. He had often
threatened to hit me, but on the day that it...it happened I had done something to displease him, I don't

know what. It didn't take much—especially when he'd been drinking,' she said flatly. 'I tried to lock myself in the bathroom but he was right behind me and I was trapped.'

Orla's voice shook as she pictured the murderous rage in David's eyes as he'd walked towards her. She'd known he was going to hit her and she remembered how her heart had thudded with dread. She only realised she was crying when Torre brushed his fingers over her cheeks to wipe away her tears.

'Go on,' he said quietly.

'He had often threatened to "slap some obedience" into me, as he put it. This time he actually struck me.' Torre's hands clasped her shoulders a little tighter but he made no comment. 'He was wearing a big gold and onyx signet ring.' In her mind she could see the ring glinting in the light as David's hand had descended. 'He hit me across the left side of my face. The ring must have had a sharp edge because it cut the skin above my eyebrow. Afterwards... I tried to stop the cut from bleeding by holding a towel over it, but it wouldn't stop, and eventually I went to the local hospital by taxi— David had drunk too much to drive, and anyway I wouldn't have asked him to take me. After the cut had been stitched I went to stay with a friend and I never went back to the house where I'd lived with David after we were married.'

'Did you report the attack to the police?' Torre frowned when she shook her head. 'Why not? Keegan had physically assaulted you and if you had reported him...'

'Who would have believed me?' she said huskily. 'David Keegan is on his way to being a national treasure, and last year he received an OBE for his charity fundraising activities. He is still regarded by many as one of the best cricket players in English sporting history. When his career hit a low point the finger of blame was pointed at me—the gold-digger wife who had married him for financial gain and broken his heart. That's what the media said about me and everyone believed *that* story.'

She stared at Torre but his features were blurred by her tears and she told herself she must have imagined the flash of pain on his face as she choked, '*You* believed the worst of me without ever asking me why I walked out of my marriage.'

She stiffened when Torre tried to pull her closer to him and she swallowed the sob that rose in her throat. 'No one would believe that David is a violent alcoholic. If I went public with what he did to me I would just be accused of being a vindictive ex-wife.'

'*Piccola*—' Torre's voice was deeper than she had ever heard it '—no woman should have to suffer domestic abuse. If you had gone to the police they would have investigated your claim, and you have evidence that Keegan threatened you in the phone and text messages he sent you. There must also be your medical notes when you went to hospital to have the cut above your eye stitched.'

'I made up a story that I had fallen and hit my head,' she muttered. She saw incomprehension in his expression and grimaced. 'I was too ashamed to admit that my husband, the man who was meant to love me, had hit me.' She hid her face in her hands and her tears dripped through her fingers. 'David said I deserved to be treated badly. He made me believe that I was useless and chipped away at my self-confidence. That is why I didn't go back to university to finish my engineering degree.'

Torre muttered something indistinct but Orla was crying too hard to make out what he had said. She did not know why she had told him the sordid details of her failed marriage and she felt utterly mortified. But when she tried to move away from him, he wrapped his arms around her and held her carefully, as if she were a delicate little thing—which of course she wasn't. She was a survivor, she reminded herself. But right now she did not feel like one, and she leaned against him and let her tears fall.

CHAPTER TEN

RAGE SWEPT THROUGH TORRE, violent and murderous in its intensity. His first instinct was to hunt down David Keegan and use his fists on the other man in the same way that Keegan had hurt Orla. He did not stop to examine the surge of protectiveness for her that pulsed a dangerous beat in his veins. He'd seen photos of the famous cricketer in the sports section of newspapers, and the idea that burly, physically powerful Keegan could have laid a finger on her, let alone struck her so hard that the resulting injury had required stitches, sickened him to his stomach.

He looked down at the top of Orla's head. She was so small and slight, a fragile rose who had been crushed, mentally and physically, by her former husband's cruelty. Her face was buried against his shirt and her body shook with the force of her sobs. He held her close, and with a huge effort of will he brought his anger with David Keegan under control.

The last thing Orla needed was yet more violence. It might satisfy a primitive urge in him to smash his fist into her ex-husband's face, but Torre knew that retribution was best served with ice-cold precision and he was determined to ruin Keegan's career and reputation.

The cricketer and celebrity had no idea of the wrath that was about to be unleashed on him, he thought grimly.

There was a knock on the door and Orla pulled out of his arms. Her eyes were wide with fear that tugged on Torre all the more because he had never seen her vulnerability before, or, if he had, he'd chosen to ignore the possibility that she was anything other than coldly grasping like her mother, he acknowledged heavily. His conscience pricked when he remembered what Orla had told him about Kimberly's damaged childhood and her recent, serious health problems.

'Does Keegan know where you live?' he asked as he crossed the room in a couple of strides.

She nodded. 'A few months ago I went on a date with a guy I knew at Mayall's. It was nothing, we just met for a drink. But after Philip dropped me home I received a particularly offensive phone call from David, warning me to stay away from other men. His obsessive jealousy was one reason why I left him.' She bit her lip. 'He probably saw the picture in the newspapers of us at the ARC centenary party and it sent him into one of his rages.'

Torre yanked the door open, every muscle in his body prepared for action, and stared at a woman with purple hair.

'*Oh!* Hi. Is Orla around?'

His breath whistled through his teeth. Glancing over his shoulder, he saw Orla hastily wipe her eyes before she joined him at the door and introduced the woman. 'This is my neighbour Mandy. Torre is my boss,' she explained to her friend. 'Do you mind if we postponed our pizza session to another time? I think I'm coming down with a cold.'

Orla had clearly been crying and Mandy looked un-convinced by the lie, but she shrugged. 'Sure. I thought you should know that your crazy ex-husband has been hanging around. I told him you were away, and he did that.' She pointed to a hole in the landing wall where a chunk of plaster was missing. 'He put his fist through the plaster.'

Orla darted a quick look at Torre. 'Mandy knows about David.'

'I'm glad you weren't here when he called,' her friend said with concern in her voice. 'He might have taken his temper out on you rather than the wall.'

After Mandy had returned to her flat on the floor below, Torre eyed Orla's white face. 'Pack a bag with whatever you need and we'll go to the hotel. Obviously you can't stay here. I'll call a lawyer friend of mine and ask him to apply to the court for a restraining order to keep Keegan away from you. But before any legal pro-cess can begin I imagine it will be necessary for you to report Keegan's harassment to the police. Have you kept all the texts he sent you?'

She hugged her arms around her. 'I don't want you to involve the police and I can't afford to pay for a lawyer.'

'You won't have to. I will take care of legal expenses.'

'No!' A flash of her old spirit returned. 'I'm not your responsibility. If there was a restraining order David might adhere to it for a while, but in a few weeks I won't be your assistant and I'll have to come back to live here. Meanwhile, you have your own life in Italy and you can't protect me for ever. I've learned that the best way to manage David is to keep my head down and try not to make him angry.'

The defeated look in her eyes evoked an emotion in

Torre that was a complicated mix of sympathy, a need to protect her and a possessiveness he did not want to examine too deeply. 'You can't live the rest of your life in fear of Keegan,' he said quietly, and felt a sensation like a hand was squeezing his heart when her mouth trembled.

'David is powerful,' she whispered.

'Not as powerful as me, *cara*.' There was deadly menace beneath the gentle tone he used to reassure her.

In the car on the way to the hotel Torre leaned his head against the backrest while the chauffeur navigated the busy London streets. A plan was forming in his mind. He would buy an apartment in London for Orla, maybe a place overlooking the river Thames with a balcony so that she could sit outside in the summer, he mused. The building would have to have round-the-clock security so he could be sure she was safe when he wasn't around.

As Chairman and CEO of his family's company he needed to be based in Italy but he could fly to London to spend weekends with her. His fascination with Orla showed no sign of fading but by providing her with a flat in London he would maintain control over their affair. If she wanted to work, as she had insisted many times that she did, he would arrange a job for her at ARC UK. Something to occupy her while he was away but that would allow her to be available whenever he wanted her.

Even as the idea came into his head, Torre realised that Orla was capable of far more than a clerical job to pass the time between his visits. For the past ten days that she had been his assistant she'd demonstrated not only an excellent work ethic but an impressive knowledge of structural engineering, and he anticipated that if she resumed studying for her BSc she would have no problem passing her final exams and qualifying as a civil engineer. All she lacked was the self-confidence that her brutal ex-husband had taken from her.

Guilt knotted in Torre's gut when he remembered Orla's accusation that he had been too ready to believe the stories in the tabloids speculating that she had married Keegan for his money. It had been convenient for him to think she was a fortune hunter because it had given him an excuse to keep away from her. But if that had been his reasoning, it had failed spectacularly.

His mouth twisted with self-derision. The simple fact was that he couldn't keep his hands off Orla. He glanced at her, huddled in the corner of the limousine. Her eyes looked too big in her pinched face and there wasn't a scrap of colour on her cheeks. Her glorious hair streamed over her shoulders and he knew it would feel like silk against his skin when they were both naked and he lifted her over him so that her hair cascaded onto his chest. Desire stirred low in his gut. He seemed to have been in a permanent state of arousal since she had burst into his life again.

But tonight she needed tenderness rather than passion, and once they had arrived at the hotel and he ushered her into their suite, he took her cold hand in his and led her into the opulent bathroom. It was a measure of how shattered she was by her ex-husband's abusive phone calls that she simply stared at him when he switched on the shower.

She blinked as if she had dragged her thoughts back from some grim place. 'You're going to take a shower? I'll leave,' she said huskily.

Torre watched a soft stain of colour wing along her exquisite cheekbones as he caught hold of the hem of her sweater and pulled the garment over her head, baring her small, firm breasts. He wanted to take them in his hands and feel their softness, taste the cherry-red nipples that adorned the creamy mounds. But what he wanted wasn't important. Tonight was all about Orla, and he set about his self-appointed task of dismissing the shadows from her eyes.

'*You* are going to have a shower, *piccola*. And I am going to take care of you.' It was odd how his words sounded like a solemn oath.

'I don't want you to take care of me,' Orla said to Torre, aware that it was the biggest lie she'd ever told. Her instincts warned her that if she allowed herself to succumb to the gentleness in his voice, which she had never heard from him before, she would be lost for ever. It truth, she was feeling lost now. David's phone call had been a painful reminder that she dared not trust her own judgement. Her marriage had been a frightening experience, and in a strange way she'd felt relieved when Torre had said he did not want a relationship with her. He only wanted sex, and the lack of emotional ties between them provided a safety net and allowed her to explore her sensuality.

Taking care of her was something completely different but the concept was dangerously beguiling. She had been pretty much independent since she'd been ten years old when her father had died and shortly after that devastating event her mother had dumped her in a boarding school because Kimberly's new lover had disliked children.

'I certainly don't need you to help me take a shower,' she told Torre, clinging to her stubbornness because it was the only thing she had left of herself. Yet there was a part of her that longed to lower her guard and let go of her reservations, to be swept away to a world of sensation and primitive passion that focused entirely on assuaging the ache that filled her body and her heart. She wanted to forget her ex-husband's vindictiveness and glory in the sweet surrender of making love with Torre. That was why, when he drew her into his arms, she stared at him with an unguarded expression in her eyes.

He made a rough sound in his throat as he pulled her into his heat and strength, into heaven. Orla did not have the willpower to argue when he knelt to remove her trainers before he peeled her jeans down her legs so that she was left in just her knickers. Torre quickly dispensed with them before stripping off his own clothes. She blushed as she stared at his naked body. He was a work of art and she allowed her gaze to roam over the defined ridges of his abdominal muscles beneath his sleek, golden skin. She moved her eyes down to the hardened length of his arousal and heard him swear.

'If you look at me like that, *cara*, I won't be responsible for my actions,' he warned her softly, and then he scooped her up into his arms and carried her into the shower. The warm spray felt like little needles hitting her skin and the invigorating power shower revived her and washed away the poison of her ex-husband's vile insults.

Torre would not allow her to do a thing, and she caught her breath as he soaped every inch of her body. His hands created havoc as he stroked his way down from her shoulders, paying careful attention to her breasts before sliding lower over her stomach and thighs.

'I think I'm clean enough,' she gasped, when he smoothed the bar of soap over her buttocks and then moved his hand round to the front and slipped it between her legs. Still he wasn't done with her, and he reached for the bottle of shampoo and washed her hair, his skilful fingers massaging her scalp and easing her tension, so that by the time he switched off the shower and wrapped her in a towel she felt boneless.

He used the hairdrier on her hair, smoothing the long, silken strands with a brush while Orla watched him in the mirror, the green flecks in her hazel eyes sparkling like emeralds when the towel he had knotted around his waist slipped dangerously low.

She assumed he would take her to bed, and he laughed softly at her disappointed expression when he exchanged her towel for a robe and donned one of the hotel's blue, monogrammed robes before he caught hold of her hand and led her to the dining area of the suite. 'Food first,' he said as he sat her on a chair in front of the table where an array of dishes had been delivered courtesy of room service.

'I'm not hungry.' There was still a knot of tension in the pit of her stomach and she doubted she would sleep tonight after her latest run-in with David. It was two years since she had left him, and more than two months since the divorce had been granted, yet he was still hounding her. She despaired that she would ever be free from the fear he induced in her.

'Try some omelette.' Torre smiled as he offered her a forkful of fluffy cheese omelette.

'You intend to feed me? I'm not a child.'

'Humour me,' he said quietly. His eyes were as soft as woodsmoke, and with a little *hmmf* sound of frustration at his bossiness she opened her mouth and ate the piece of omelette. He fed her four more forkfuls and when she indicated that she'd eaten enough, he held a glass of sparkling rosé wine to her lips while she took a couple of sips. It was pathetic how her heart responded to his kindness, Orla thought. She could become addicted to the feeling of being cherished.

It wasn't real, she reminded herself. In a few weeks her role as Torre's assistant—and their personal relationship that he insisted wasn't one—would end. But just for a little while it was nice to believe in the tender promise of his kiss when he carried her into the bedroom, removed her robe and placed her between the crisp white sheets.

He slid into bed beside her and pulled her into his arms, but when she moved her hand between their bodies, he stopped her and caught hold of her wrists, lifting her hands behind her head.

'Believe me, your ex-husband will never hurt you, physically or verbally, again, *piccola*,' he told her in a grimly determined voice that caused her to release her breath on a shaky sigh. 'I made a number of phone calls while you ran down to give your neighbour a spare key to your flat. David Keegan is under no illusions that if he attempts to contact you, the police and the tabloids will be tipped off about an illegal betting syndicate that he has been involved in.'

He bent his head and brushed away a tear from her cheek with his lips. 'It's over,' he said gently. 'Keegan is in your past and you can look to the future without fear.'

Relief poured through her. It was hard to accept that the nightmare was truly over, but she *did* believe Torre. His determination to protect her made it impossible for her to fight the truth any longer. She loved him. She always had, and she could not imagine a time when he would not fill her heart.

Dared she believe that the tender, caring side to him that he had shown her tonight meant he felt something for her? The past was behind her and the future was no more than a tantalising hope that she would be a fool to put all her faith in. Only the present was certain. *Now* she was in a very big bed with Torre, and the gleam of molten silver in his eyes sent a shiver of anticipation through her as he held her wrists above her head and bent his head to her breast.

He used his tongue to caress her body with the same attention to detail that he had used his hands and a bar of soap in the shower. The lash of his tongue across her nipples soon had her writhing, and when he drew each turgid peak in turn into his mouth and sucked, she moaned and arched her hips as sweet sensation poured like liquid honey through her veins. She heard his husky laughter when he freed her wrists and she gripped his shoulders, digging her fingernails into his skin as he shifted down her body and nudged her thighs apart.

The feel of his mouth *there* at the heart of her femininity almost sent her over the edge and she sank her fingers into his hair and tugged, hard, until he lifted his head.

'Don't you like what I'm doing to you, *gattina*?' There was still that deep, sexy laughter in his voice, a suggestion of his glorious arrogance because he knew full well that she loved it when he pleasured her with his wickedly inventive tongue.

'I like it too much,' she panted. 'But I want you inside me. I need you, Torre.' Too late she realised how the word *need* betrayed her. An indefinable expression flashed in his eyes, but then he lifted himself over her and possessed her with one hard thrust, followed by another and another so that she forgot everything but the beauty of their two bodies moving in perfect accord. It couldn't last, and they reached the highest peak together, hovered there for timeless seconds before freefalling over the edge of the precipice into the shuddering ecstasy of their simultaneous release.

Torre waited until the sound of Orla's even breaths told him she had fallen asleep before he eased his arm from around her so that her head slipped off his chest onto the pillow. She stirred, and her gold eyelashes fluttered before fanning out on her cheeks. In the lamplight the thin red scar above her eyebrow was noticeable on her pale skin. He guessed that she usually disguised it with make-up.

His jaw clenched. A few days ago he had already begun to investigate her ex-husband before Orla had admitted the extent of David Keegan's brutality. By calling in a few favours, it had been remarkably easy to dig up dirt on Keegan, and if the story of his betting scam operation was leaked to the press the famous cricketer would be exposed as the scumbag he really was. Torre would have preferred Orla to have received justice for Keegan's bad treatment of her, but at least this way she was spared the trauma of facing her ex-husband in a courtroom.

She rolled over in the bed and the sheet slipped down, exposing one white breast tipped with a dusky-pink nipple. Predictably he felt himself harden but he resisted the urge to slide back beneath the sheets and take the slow and sensual route to nirvana this time. He could not comprehend what was wrong with him. Sure, he had a healthy sex drive but this *obsession* with Orla had to stop. He did not want to want her so much that she was on his mind all the time. Hell, he wanted his life back—his comfortable life that he had been in control of before she had arrived with the destructive force of a tornado and blown him apart.

All that rubbish she'd spouted in the car earlier, suggesting he feared forming close relationships because his mother had died when he was a young boy. *Dio*, he had not been affected by his mother's death, he'd just blocked out his thoughts of her and he hadn't ever talked about her because what was the point? Talking wouldn't have brought her back.

What he had learned when he was six years old was that no one could control events such as death. It was only possible to control how you dealt with painful emotions like sadness and grief. As a young boy his logical brain had worked out that if you did not love anyone then you would not run the risk of being hurt. But Orla's suggestion that he *feared* love was ridiculous.

It was true that he had become engaged to Marisa when he hadn't been in love with her. To his mind it had seemed eminently sensible in light of rising divorce rates to base marriage on mutual respect and shared goals rather than the unstable emotion that love too often proved to be. Torre raked his hands through his hair, feeling uncomfortable with the idea that he had decided to have a loveless marriage to protect himself from the pain he associated with love. But it hadn't happened because Marisa had fallen in love, prompting the end of their engagement.

Swearing beneath his breath, he walked noiselessly from the bedroom into the lounge, located his tablet and entered a search for luxury properties in central London. It was time he took back control of the situation with Orla. In a few weeks Renzo would return to work as his assistant and Torre was confident that when he was no longer spending every day with Orla, like he did now, the disturbing hold she had over him would disappear.

He would set her up in an apartment and give her one of his credit cards so that she could buy some new clothes. Pretty dresses and sexy underwear purchased for his delectation, he mused. It was standard stuff he'd done with previous mistresses, and there would be rules, boundaries—not this permanent hunger for her that demeaned him because he couldn't control it.

Satisfied with his plan, he scrolled through the property listings and requested to be sent more information on a few of them.

CHAPTER ELEVEN

'DO YOU WANT to eat in tonight or shall we go out for dinner?' Torre asked one evening. 'We could drive along the coast to Positano and have a meal at the seafood restaurant down by the harbour that you liked when we went there a couple of weeks ago.'

Orla experienced a sudden queasy sensation at the thought of eating fish. 'I'd rather have dinner at home,' she said quickly. 'I'll cook. I know my cooking doesn't come anywhere near to your housekeeper's standard, but Tomas and Silvia will be away for a few more days, and we can't eat out every night.'

'All right. But if you cook, I'll do the dishes. That way it's a fair division of labour.'

'Loading the dishwasher is hardly labour intensive,' she teased.

Torre grinned. 'I need to save my energy for tonight, *cara*.'

Orla glanced at him sitting beside her in the car and her heart gave its usual flip because he was just so gorgeous. They drove the fifty-minute journey between Casa Elisabetta and his office in Naples most days, although when they went to ARC's headquarters in Rome they travelled by helicopter.

Torre's tanned hands held the steering wheel loosely as he drove the car with consummate skill along the winding road from Naples back to Ravello. He had put the sunroof down and the breeze ruffled his dark hair. Every day after work he pulled off his jacket and tie and undid the top three or four of his shirt buttons before he climbed into the car. It was a signal that the serious stuff was done and now it was time to relax and have fun.

The mellow days of late summer on the Amalfi Coast had slipped past, and a month had gone by since they had left London following their visit to the new Docklands development managed by ARC UK. Since then they had been to ARC construction projects in France and Hong Kong. Orla's interest in engineering was stronger than ever, and with her new self-confidence, which stemmed from Torre's belief in her capabilities, she had applied to her old university to complete her degree. She planned to study part time so that she could look for a secretarial job in London until she qualified as a civil engineer.

She was still committed to paying for her mother's medical bills but Kimberly's health had improved enough for her to be able to move into a house in Chicago which her new husband had adapted to accommodate a wheelchair. Free from the worry of her mother and her ex-husband—she hadn't received a single call or text from David, whose popularity with the public had slipped after he had crashed his car while he'd been drunk—Orla tried to convince herself that she had plenty to look forward to when her temporary job as Torre's assistant finished in two weeks' time.

He had not mentioned what would happen to them when his assistant Renzo returned. And the truth was

that there was no *them*—not in the way she would like
there to be, she thought bleakly. They made love every
night with a wildfire passion that blazed hotter than
ever. But for Torre it was just sex. Orla knew he would
never fall in love with her and she was convinced that
he was still in love with his ex-fiancée.

She would miss the companionship they had shared
for the past month, she acknowledged with a heavy
heart. Everything—eating meals with him, swimming
in the pool together after a day at work, watching a
film with him in the cinema room. She had harboured
a fragile hope that they might have a future, that the
way he stroked her hair when they lay in each other's
arms after making love might mean he felt something
for her other than lust. But this morning when they'd
had breakfast outside on the terrace, as they usually
did, while glancing through the daily newspapers, her
silly romantic dream had hit—*slam*—a concrete wall
of reality.

The picture on an inside page of one of the papers
had been innocuous enough—a stunningly beautiful
woman, a handsome man and an adorable baby. The
caption beneath the photo had caught Orla's attention.
Translated into English it said: *Count Valetti's daughter Marisa Cardello and her husband Giovanni show
off their new daughter Lucia.*

'Cute baby,' she'd commented to Torre. And it had
been then, when he had taken the newspaper from her
and stared at the photo as if he'd seen a ghost, that she'd
realised the woman was *his* Marisa, his ex-fiancée who,
according to Jules, had broken off the engagement and
broken Torre's heart.

'I suppose all children are deemed to be cute—at

least by their parents,' he'd drawled as he had handed the newspaper back to her. 'I must admit that my knowledge of babies is based on what some of my friends who have had fatherhood thrust upon them have told me.'

Orla had been puzzled. 'What do you mean?'

'Gennaro and Stephan's girlfriends both fell pregnant by accident—supposedly,' Torre had said sardonically. 'In each case the couple married for the sake of the child, but neither of my friends are happy in their respective marriages, and I suspect they felt that they had been trapped in a situation they had not wished for.'

'It takes two people to make a baby,' Orla had pointed out. 'Perhaps your friends should have been more careful.'

'And perhaps their girlfriends saw pregnancy as a quick route down the aisle,' he had countered, making her shake her head.

'Why are you so cynical?'

He had shrugged. 'I'm a realist. There are some women who would deliberately fall pregnant to force the baby's father to marry them.'

The conversation had moved onto a less contentious subject after that, but at work later that day Torre had been uncommunicative—although once or twice Orla had looked up from her desk to find him standing in the doorway linking their two offices, watching her with a closed expression on his face that had made her think he was comparing her unexciting paleness with his ex-fiancée Marisa's sultry beauty.

Now, as he turned the car through the gates of Casa Elisabetta, Orla looked up at the ultra-contemporary building that never ceased to fascinate her with its bold design. 'Why did you build such a huge house when most of the time only you live in it?' she asked him.

'I don't anticipate I'll live alone for ever,' he said as he climbed out of the car.

'Did you design your home with someone in mind who you hoped would share it with you?' She knew that construction of the villa had begun while he had been engaged to Marisa and it occurred to her that the house might be a spectacular monument to the woman he loved, in the same way that the Taj Mahal in India was synonymous with everlasting love.

Torre paused on the front steps, his jacket slung over his shoulder and his sunglasses hiding the expression in his eyes. 'I suppose I did,' he said. There was an odd note in his voice that Orla could not define. 'Where are you going?' he called after her when she turned and began to walk back up the drive.

'I told you this morning that I have a doctor's appointment. I hope to find out why I keep feeling nauseous after eating meals. It's probably an intolerance to a certain food. I really hope I don't have to give up pasta, although it might be a good thing for my hips,' she said ruefully, thinking about the few pounds she'd gained recently.

'You should have reminded me. Get in the car and I'll drive you into Ravello.'

She kept on walking, not wanting Torre to see the tears in her eyes because she was sure he had built his amazing house for the woman he loved. 'I'd rather walk, after sitting in the car for nearly an hour. And you are expecting a phone call from the Shanghai office,' she reminded him.

In truth, Orla wanted some time alone. The scene

at breakfast had bothered her for the rest of the day. Torre's reaction to the photograph of his ex-fiancée had filled her with despair, but the discussion they'd had when he had told her about his two friends who had reluctantly married their girlfriends as a result of unplanned pregnancies had triggered a niggling concern in her mind.

The nauseous feeling she had been experiencing recently happened after she had eaten a meal, but for the past few days she had also felt sick first thing in the morning. Her period was only two days late, and it was highly unlikely, if not impossible for her to have fallen pregnant when she had been taking the Pill for the past three years, she reassured herself. There hadn't been a chance for her to slip out of the office during the day to visit a chemist and buy a pregnancy test, but she had phoned the doctor's surgery and made an appointment because she needed a new supply of her contraceptive Pill, and she decided to mention that she had been feeling more tired than usual lately.

Ravello was a popular town on the Amalfi Coast, and even though it was the end of the summer the narrow streets were filled with tourists. Usually Orla loved the bustle of the place, but when she emerged from the doctor's surgery she headed for a quiet spot away from the crowds. The famous gardens of Villa Cimbrone were open to the public but luckily there was no one else around when she stood on the terrace lined with white marble busts and stared out over the bay. But she did not notice the breath-taking beauty of the view. She was numb with shock after a pregnancy test at the doctor's surgery had proved positive.

'I *can't* be pregnant,' she'd said shakily. Her first re-action had been one of panic and utter disbelief. 'I have never missed taking a Pill.'

'Have you been unwell at all in the last couple of months?' the doctor asked.

'No. Well—I did have a stomach upset, but it only lasted for forty-eight hours.' She remembered that she'd been worried she would be too unwell to travel to Amalfi for Giuseppe's birthday party.

'Missing just one or two Pills or, as in your case, being sick for a few days could have lessened the ef-fectiveness of the contraceptive Pill,' the doctor had re-minded her. That was when Orla's panic had turned to fear. She knew the Pill could only be relied on to pre-vent an unplanned pregnancy if it was taken regularly, but when she had made love with Torre she had been swept away by their tumultuous passion and she'd to-tally forgotten to take extra precautions.

She leaned against the railings on the balcony of Villa Cimbrone and tried to calm herself, but there was no escaping the fact that it was a disaster. She was ex-pecting Torre's baby and the conversation they'd had that very morning gave her an indication of how he was likely to react to her news. Some of his old cyni-cism had returned when he had told her of his friends who had both felt trapped when their girlfriends had fallen pregnant.

Would Torre think that she had deliberately con-ceived his child? She felt sick as she tried to imagine his response when she told him he was going to be a father. Would he lose his temper, like her ex-husband had done when she'd told David that her period was ten

days late? Memories swamped her mind. It had been
in the first few months of her marriage and although
she had already grown wary of David's unpredictable
mood swings, he had not yet displayed his violent temper. They had been on his friend's yacht, cruising the
Mediterranean, and Orla hadn't been able to take a pregnancy test but she had mentioned her suspicion that she
was pregnant.

David had stayed silent for so long that she had felt
increasingly nervous. His face had twisted in an ugly
expression. 'You stupid cow. I told you when we got
married that I don't want children while I'm focusing
on my career.'

'It was an accident. I didn't mean it to happen.' She
had sought to defend herself.

'You'll have to get rid of it,' David had told her
coldly, and his shocking statement had made her realise that any feelings she might have had for him had
died. Later the same day her period had started and
she'd felt relieved.

But this time her pregnancy had been confirmed. Her
hand crept to her stomach as she tried to comprehend
the enormity of what had happened—what was happening inside her now—a new life developing. Her baby,
who she would love and protect with her own life if
necessary, she vowed as maternal instinct replaced her
shock at the prospect that she was going to be a mother.

Briefly she considered not telling Torre. If, as seemed
likely, he intended their relationship to end when her role
as his temporary assistant finished then it might be better
to keep her news to herself. But she quickly dismissed
the idea. She had no idea how he would feel about her
being pregnant but he had proved over and over again

that he was nothing like her ex-husband. And the baby would need its father just as she had needed her father. She had to hope and trust that Torre would want his child.

On the walk back to Casa Elisabetta, Orla rehearsed how she was going to break the news to Torre but her heart was thudding so hard that she was surprised she could not hear it when she located him in his study. He was working at his desk but he looked up when she entered the room and immediately switched off his computer.

'Hello, *cara*.' He smiled as he walked over to where she stood in the doorway, her tension ratcheting up by the second. It did not help that he looked devastatingly sexy in a pair of faded jeans that sat low on his hips and a black tee shirt moulding his muscular chest. He pushed a hand through his swathe of dark hair and the gleam in his grey eyes almost reassured her that she wasn't standing at the edge of an abyss—almost.

'You were a long time at the doctor's. I was starting to worry,' he murmured, before he covered her mouth with his. The kiss stole her breath and Orla thought that she would give her life to keep this moment enshrined for ever. But her life was not her own any more—she had her baby to consider, to love. That thought filled her with fierce joy and an even fiercer resolve.

Torre lifted his head and looked down at her, a faint frown of concern drawing his brows together. 'Was everything all right at the doctor's?'

'Yes…well—no. What I mean is…' She took a deep breath and sent up a silent prayer, aware that her future and, more importantly, her baby's future hinged on this pivotal moment and Torre's reaction to her news.

'Orla?'

'I'm having your baby.' The words burst from her lips and came direct from her heart. However Torre chose to respond made no difference to the unassailable fact that she had every intention of going ahead with her pregnancy. The memory of how David had reacted to her suspected pregnancy haunted her. And Torre's initial reaction—or rather his complete lack of reaction—was not a good sign, she thought, feeling a heavy sense of dread in the pit of her stomach.

He was so still that he could have been a statue carved out of granite. Only a nerve jumping in his cheek told her that he hadn't turned to stone, and his eyes had lost their smoky warmth and were as hard and cold as steel. Ice formed around her heart. It was David all over again—only this time there really was a baby.

'Say *something* at least,' she choked. The man who had been her lover and, yes, her friend for the past weeks had turned into a stranger. But she had been fooling herself, Orla thought bleakly. Torre had always kept a part of himself distant from her and as he continued to stare at her with no expression at all in his eyes she sensed that he was bringing the shutters down and she would never be able to reach him.

'What do you want me to say?' His voice was carefully controlled and somehow that made him seem more forbidding than if he had shouted and stormed at her. She could cope with his anger. But his apparent lack of interest in the child they had created together told her everything she needed to know about their relationship, and the fragile hope she had nurtured withered and died.

Torre did not know how to deal with the wildness that swept through him, or the knowledge that *this* would be his life from now on. Out of his control and at the mercy of emotions that he had never sought nor wanted.

What he wanted was his well-ordered life where there were no nasty surprises that inevitably brought hurt and pain. He remembered the ache in his chest like his heart was about to explode when he had touched his mother's cold hand and realised that this was what death did. His *mamma* would never smile at him or hold him in her arms ever again.

He had understood the fragility of life when he was six years old and he had learned that love hurt. He'd managed perfectly well without that pernicious emotion since he was a boy, but now events had spun out of his control. Orla was pregnant with his child. He felt something like panic—he refused to call it fear. And he was furious because he had never asked for this, for *her*.

Ever since Orla had swept into his life he had broken every rule he lived by. He didn't know how to react to the latest bomb she'd detonated and anger was his only defence against all the other emotions roaring through him.

'You told me you were on the Pill.'

She flinched, and he saw something flicker across her face that looked like disappointment with him, as if he'd failed her. It wouldn't be the first time, his conscience whispered.

'I *am* on the Pill, but it didn't work. I had a stomach upset a few days before I came to Amalfi for Giuseppe's birthday party.' She hesitated and bit her lip. 'I should have remembered that a bout of sickness can lessen the Pill's effectiveness. I can only assume I wasn't protected when we made lo—had sex on my first night in Amalfi. The test showed that I am approximately six weeks pregnant.' She lifted her chin and he saw determination and something like a challenge in her eyes. 'I accept responsibility. It was my mistake. I only told you about the baby because you have a right to know.'

Torre walked back to his desk and lowered himself onto the chair. It was familiar territory for him to be behind a desk, in control. According to Orla, she had only told him about her pregnancy because it was his right to know. *Dio.* His jaw clenched. Did she think he was going to abandon his child? It was his duty to provide financial security for Orla and the baby. But a child would need more than money, his conscience insisted. Providing money was the easy bit. A child required love—the very thing that Torre had assiduously avoided for most of his life.

Orla had followed him across the room and she stood in front of the desk, watching him with a wary expression that tugged on the huge great *thing* inside him that was lodged beneath his ribs and made breathing painful. He could not deal with the thing, the swirl of emotions that he didn't want, that he'd never wanted. Instead he focused on practicalities.

Some of the property details that he had requested from an exclusive estate agency in London were on the desk and he picked them up and held them out to Orla. 'I had already decided to buy an apartment for you when your temporary role as my assistant finishes,' he said coolly. 'You may as well look through the listings and choose a place that you think will be suitable for you and the child.'

Colour flared on her cheeks and then drained away, leaving her looking pale and hurt, Torre noted with a stab of guilt. He wondered if she was feeling well, if the baby was healthy. It wasn't even a baby at this stage, he reminded himself. It was a collection of cells, yet already he was concerned for the new life that he and Orla had created together.

'I don't want a fancy apartment,' she said stiffly. 'I would never allow you to pay for me.'

He frowned. Surely she knew that she was his responsibility now? 'You can hardly bring up a child in the rabbit hutch you currently live in.'

'I'll manage.'

'I don't want you to have to manage. I am a wealthy man and I can afford to buy you a house and everything that you and the child will need.'

Orla shook her head. 'Don't you dare suggest that I want your money.' She slammed her hands down on the desk. Her eyes flashed with fiery brilliance, and when she pushed her long hair back over her shoulders it practically crackled with fury. She was magnificently angry, and a still-functioning part of Torre's brain realised it was a sign she trusted him that she was able to give rein to her temper after her ex-husband had destroyed her self-confidence.

'The only thing I want is for you to tell me how you feel about my pregnancy, and what, if any, involvement you intend to have with your child…' her voice shook '…and with me.'

Torre did not know how to answer her. He stared at her across the desk and the truth hit him like a thunderbolt. He closed his eyes so that Orla would not see what he had denied for so long, what he was afraid of admitting to himself or to her—because he was a coward.

That thought was worse than any other in the tangled mess inside his head. He had a choice, he realised. He could fight to claim Orla, or he could watch her walk away from him and take his child with her. The first option carried the risk of pain as terrible as he'd felt when he was a boy and his mother had died. Life did not come with guarantees. But the second option, to let Orla go, was agonising.

His eyes flew open and he prepared to open his heart. But he was too late. She had gone.

CHAPTER TWELVE

IT OCCURRED TO Orla as she sat on the bus which rumbled along the winding road from Ravello down to Amalfi that she was in some sort of hideous time warp. Eight years ago, when she had fled from Torre after his crushing rejection, she had jumped onto the bus that had stopped on the main road close to the driveway of his house. A few minutes ago she had done exactly the same thing after she had run out of Casa Elisabetta. Luckily she had grabbed her handbag containing her passport and credit card on her way out of the door.

She placed her hand on her stomach, instinctively wanting to protect her baby from the upset and heartbreak that was an inevitable consequence of getting involved with Torre. It wouldn't happen again, she vowed. She needed to stay angry with him to stop herself from crying, and remembering his offer to buy an apartment in London for her made her seethe. But it made her want to cry too. Clearly he had no plans to be involved with his baby other than to provide financial support.

Her pride refused to accept anything from him. He hadn't accused her of deliberately falling pregnant to trap him, but he probably thought it, just as he had believed she was a gold-digger when they had first met.

She wondered if his offer to buy her somewhere to live had been a test, and the thought made her want to cry even more. All she had ever wanted was a relationship with him where they were both equal and that encompassed respect and friendship—and love.

Across the aisle of the bus, a little boy sitting with a woman who Orla supposed was his mother suddenly pressed his face against the window and pointed excitedly. Orla heard the roar of a car overtaking the bus and guessed that most small boys loved fast cars. She was more interested in the baby in the woman's arms. The infant was very young, perhaps only a few weeks old, and had a mass of black hair poking out from the shawl in which it was wrapped.

It was likely that her baby would have dark hair like its father, she thought, and quickly pressed her knuckles against her mouth to hold back the sob that rose in her throat. For the baby's sake she needed to stay strong.

The bus pulled into the main square in Amalfi town beside the harbour. From here, Orla knew she could take another bus to Naples airport and then book onto a flight to London. There was no point indulging in self-pity, she told herself sternly. She had already come through so much, and being a single mother would be another challenge, but she'd cope because she did not have any option.

The reason for the excitement of the boy on the bus soon became clear when Orla looked across the square at the scarlet sports car that had attracted a small crowd of admirers around it. She despised herself for the way her heart leapt at the sight of Torre leaning against his car. He looked relaxed and not at all like he had just been told he was going to be a father, perhaps because he simply did not care, she thought with a flash of bitterness. But if that was the case, why had he followed her here?

Her heart kicked against her ribs when she realised that he was watching her intently. She had to walk past him to reach the ticket office where she could buy a ticket for the Naples bus. As she drew level with him she kept her eyes fixed firmly ahead.

'Orla.' His voice was as deep as an ocean. *'Piccola.'*

She spun round to face him. 'Don't you dare *piccola* me! I don't know why you're here. I've informed you about the baby and you made it clear that you're not interested. I have nothing more to say to you.'

'But I have something to say to you,' he said in an oddly tense voice.

'I don't want to hear whatever it is. No doubt it will be some horrible accusation or other.' She was annoyed with herself when her voice shook.

He put his hand on her arm. It was only a light touch but it felt like it burned through her skin down to her bones. 'I am not going to accuse you of anything,' he said quietly. 'I thought we had moved on from the mistakes I made in the past and I hoped that I had earned your trust.'

The idea that he sounded hurt was ridiculous, Orla told herself. You couldn't hurt granite.

'To set the record straight, I never said I am not interested in our child.' He closed his fingers around her arm and she tried to shrug him off, but she'd heard rough velvet in his voice when he'd said *our child* and the ice around her heart started to melt.

The crowd that had gathered around the Ferrari were looking at them curiously. 'Orla.' The desperation in

Torre's voice startled her. 'Come home with me. *Please*. I am fully aware that my reaction when you told me of your pregnancy was not what you might have wished.'

Home had such a lovely sound to it. But Torre had built Casa Elisabetta for the woman he loved, not for her. 'I suppose I should be grateful that you offered to financially support me and the baby,' she said flatly, 'but you really don't have to worry. I'll be fine.' Quite how she would manage to hold down a job and bring up a child she hadn't yet worked out, but plenty of other women managed it, Orla told herself.

He swore softly. 'I realise I deserve to grovel on my knees before you could even consider whether you will forgive the crass way I handled your announcement.' He looked intently at her and there was nothing mocking or cynical in his eyes, which were the dull, dark grey of storm clouds. 'I'm happy to do my grovelling right here in front of an audience if that's what it will take for you to hear me out.'

She looked at him helplessly and wished she didn't love him. He deserved for her to walk away and refuse to allow him anywhere near his child, but of course she would never do that. The baby would need its father just as she had needed hers.

With a faint shrug she walked around to the passenger side of the car and lowered herself onto the leather seat. Torre slid behind the wheel and moments later they were on the road that wound up the mountain to Ravello. Neither of them spoke, and by the time he ushered her into Casa Elisabetta and led her into the sitting room, Orla's nerves were stretched to snapping point. She sank down onto the sofa before her legs gave way and watched Torre walk over to the window.

He thrust his hands into his pockets and even from a distance she sensed his edginess. 'You were right when you guessed that the trauma of my mother's death when I was young affected me badly,' he said abruptly.

'I was taken to see her in the chapel before she was buried.' He gave a grim laugh. 'To be honest, I was terrified. She was cold and grey and even at six years old I understood the finality of death. Not long after she died, my pet dog was killed. It ran into the road and was hit by a car, and I saw it happen.'

He shrugged. 'My father said it was just a dog and we could get another one, but I didn't see the point in loving something else or someone else when there was a risk I could lose them too.'

He turned around to face her, his features as expressionless as his voice. Only the nerve flickering in his cheek indicated that he was under intolerable emotional strain. 'The lessons I learned as a young boy stayed with me into adulthood. Perhaps if I'd had an opportunity to talk about my mother and grieve for her properly... I don't know, maybe I would be a different person.'

Orla nodded. 'After my father died I still went to Ireland every summer to stay with my grandmother. Nanna used tell me about my dad when he was a boy, how he was a dreamer who used to write beautiful poetry. He wrote some poems for me, and when I read them now I feel close to him.'

She hesitated. 'I understand how the loss of your mother made you wary of forming attachments, but you got engaged and presumably you were in love with Marisa Valetti. You must have been upset when she broke off your engagement?'

'Marisa didn't end our relationship, *I* did. And I was

never in love with her. I liked her, and there were some business advantages to linking our families.'

'Then why did you look so...*devastated* when you saw the picture in the paper this morning of your ex-fiancée with her husband and baby?'

'I wasn't devastated. Rather I felt a mixture of guilt and relief that Marisa had found the happiness she deserves.' His jaw tightened. 'I broke up with Marisa when I realised that she had fallen in love with me. I knew I would never return her feelings and it was only fair to end our engagement so that she could meet someone who would love her.'

Orla stared at him. 'But I thought you built this house for her. You said you had imagined living here with someone, and I assumed you meant Marisa. So who *did* you picture sharing the house and your life with?' She swallowed. 'It's clear to see that you put a huge amount of thought and attention to every detail into the design and construction of this house. It is a visual expression of love.'

Torre didn't answer, and Orla told herself she was glad because she did not think she could bear to hear the name of the woman he loved. What a mess, she thought wearily. She loved Torre, but his heart belonged to another woman, and to complicate the situation even more there was going to be a baby.

'I built the house for you.'

She jerked her head up, certain when she saw his hard, unsmiling face that she had misheard him or misunderstood. He *can't* have meant it, yet her heart persisted in thudding so hard she could barely breathe.

'Let's not play any more games, Torre. If you think you have to flatter me so that I will give you access to the baby, don't worry. I would never stop you from seeing your child. Why would you have built this house for me? You despised me.' Her voice shook.

He gave a jolt as if she had slapped him, and his face was no longer expressionless when he strode over to her, caught hold of her by her upper arms and pulled her to her feet.

'I never despised you. *Dio*, don't cry, *piccola*,' he said roughly, brushing away the tears on her cheeks with his thumbs. 'I'm more sorry than I can say for the way I reacted when you told me about the baby. I was…' He swallowed convulsively and Orla's heart stopped when she saw the brilliant sheen in his eyes.

'Torre?'

'I was scared,' he gritted. 'I *am* scared.' He gave her a crooked smile that made her hurt and made her hope. 'I was a coward, Orla. I never wanted to fall in love. My father was distraught when my mother died. Years later I watched Giuseppe tie himself in knots over your mother and in my stupid arrogance I thought he was a fool. But then I saw you and every defence I'd built up since I was six years old came crashing down. I had never wanted any woman the way I wanted you, and when I discovered that you were a virgin it felt like fate. It felt like you were mine.'

He sighed heavily. 'When I found out who you were, it gave me an excuse to send you away, to tell myself that you were the same as your mother. But as hard as I tried to forget you, I couldn't. One day I was standing on the site of the old farmhouse, which had been demolished, and I saw clearly in my mind the villa I wanted to build.'

He slipped his hand beneath her chin and tilted her

face up to meet his fierce gaze. 'I saw you, us, our children, and I knew that the only person I wanted to share the house and my life with was you.'

She shook her head. It had to be a cruel joke and she would not allow herself to believe him. 'How can you say these things when you were planning to keep me as your mistress in a London apartment before you knew I was pregnant?' Of everything he had done, that was the most hurtful. 'You won't want me in a few months when I'm heavily pregnant and fat and ugly.' Some of her old self-doubt returned.

'I will want you always and for ever.' His voice was so solemn that Orla almost forgot to breathe. He moved his hands from her arms to her still-slender waist, which, of course, bore no sign yet of the miracle taking place within her. 'You will always be beautiful, *cara mia*, but never more so than when you are big with our child growing inside you.'

He ran his fingers lightly down her cheek. 'Before I knew about your pregnancy I had decided to move my headquarters from Italy to London for a year, partly so that I can be involved in the Docklands project, but mainly because I knew you had applied to go back to university to finish your degree. I'd planned to lease an apartment for us to live in. Incidentally there is no reason why you can't study for your civil engineering qualifications while you are pregnant.'

He tucked a lock of her hair behind her ear with a hand that shook a little. 'Orla…' He breathed her name like a prayer. 'I love you and it terrifies the hell out of me because I don't know how I would survive if I lost you. But I can't fight the way I feel any more,' he said thickly. 'I used to think that if I never loved then I would never be hurt, but I am so deeply in love with you and it's killing me not knowing if I have destroyed any chance I might have had with you. When you walked out of here earlier I knew I couldn't let you go again. The truth is that I should never have let you go eight years ago.'

'Oh, Torre,' she whispered, disbelief turning to wonder and then utter joy. Through her tears she saw that his lashes were wet, and with a soft cry she wrapped her arms around his waist and held him tight. 'I love you with all my heart. I always have and I always will,' she said simply.

He tightened his arms around her and buried his face against her neck. She felt dampness against her skin, and her heart turned over because she knew they were the tears of a young boy who had never cried. And then he kissed her; a slow, sweet kiss at first, and then, as the fire ignited between them, she pressed her body to his and heard him give a low groan.

'*Ti amo*, Orla. Will you marry me and let me take care of you and our baby, the children I hope we will have in the future?'

'Yes,' she said fearlessly. Her eyes were bright with love and there was not a flicker of doubt in her voice because she knew she belonged with Torre, just as he belonged with her. He had built them a wonderful house, but home would be wherever they were together.

'I love you,' Torre whispered against her lips, before kissing her again. 'I have never said those words to anyone before,' he admitted when he carried her up to their bedroom and laid her down on the bed.

He undressed her and then himself and his hands shook slightly when he lay down next to her and

smoothed her hair back from her face. Orla caught
her breath as he stroked her breasts and then lowered
his head to take one nipple and then the other into his
mouth. 'I love you,' he said again, and his voice was so
gentle, so *loving* that tears filled her eyes.

'I will tell you every day how much I adore you,' he
promised. 'When you left, I was scared that I had lost
you for ever.'

Orla put her hands on either side of his face and
drew his mouth down to hers. 'You couldn't lose me
because I am yours, and you are mine,' she said softly.
And Torre realised that it was as simple and as earth-
shattering as that.

He told her that he loved her as he moved over her
and joined their bodies as one. Their passion was as
fierce as ever but there was tenderness too, and a deep,
abiding love that would last a lifetime.

Two hearts bound together. For ever.

They were married a month later in the exquisitely beautiful Duomo in Ravello, in front of family and friends,
and after the ceremony they walked down the steps of
the church into the *piazza* and it seemed as though all
the people of the town had gathered to wish them well.

Torre had felt as though his heart would explode
when he'd turned his head and watched Orla walk down
the aisle towards him. Wearing a simple white silk and
lace wedding gown and with her pale red hair loose, she
had carried a bouquet of white roses and her only jewellery, apart from the teardrop diamond ring that he had
given her for an engagement ring, was the gold-plated
chain and four-leaf clover pendant from her father.

Fourteen months later, Torre once again felt his heart

swell with love and pride as he watched his wife walk onto the stage at the university's graduation ceremony to receive her degree in civil engineering.

'Can you see your *mamma*?' he murmured to his son, pointing to the stage where Orla, dressed in her academic robes, stood with the other graduates. Six-month-old Luca grinned, showing his first tooth, and Torre swallowed hard and kissed the baby's silky black curls. The baby was adored by his parents, and Torre gave thanks every day for the two miracles in his life.

Life could not be more perfect, he said to Orla a week after she had graduated and they returned to Casa Elisabetta—the house that Torre had built for the woman who had captured his heart, and was named after the only other woman he had loved. 'Have you decided if you want to take on a civil engineering role at ARC, or do you want to wait until Luca is a bit older before you focus on your career?'

'My career will have to wait a little longer.' She looped her arms around his neck, and he pulled her close, burying his face in her silky hair. 'When you built the house and you imagined us living here with our children, how many children did you picture?' she asked him.

He drew back a little and gave her a puzzled look. 'I don't know. Five or six.' He laughed at her startled expression. 'I didn't see an exact number, I only had eyes for you, *amore mio*.'

'Well, I'm not sure about six children, but baby number two is going to arrive earlier than we'd planned. It seems that we are a very potent combination,' she said ruefully.

Torre contained his fierce sense of joy and searched

her face. 'How do you feel about having another baby? I know we said we would like to give Luca a brother or sister, but you studied hard for your degree, and we were going to wait for a year or so to give you time to enjoy your career before adding to our family.'

Her smile stole his breath, as it always did. 'I'm overjoyed to be pregnant again,' she said simply. 'I will love the new baby with all my heart, as I love Luca, and one day I'll love working in an engineering role. But more than anything else, I love you, Torre.'

He swallowed hard and wasn't ashamed of the sudden brightness in his eyes. 'And I love you,' he said softly. 'Always.'

* * * * *

IMPRISONED BY THE
GREEK'S RING
Caitlin Crews

Atlas was a primitive man, when all was said and done. And whatever else happened in this dirty game, Lexi was his.

Entirely his, to do with as he wished.

He kissed her and he kissed her. He indulged himself. He toyed with her. He tasted her. He was unapologetic and thorough at once.

And with every taste, every indulgence, Atlas felt.

He felt.

He, who hadn't felt a damned thing in years. He, who had walled himself off to survive. He had become stone. Fury in human form.

But Lexi tasted like hope.

"This doesn't feel like revenge," she whispered in his ear, and she sounded drugged.

"I'm delighted you think so," he replied.

And then he set his mouth to hers again, because it was easier. Or better. Or simply because he had to, or die wanting her.

Lexi thrashed beneath him, and he wasn't sure why until he tilted back his head to get a better look at her face. And the answer slammed through him like some kind of cannon-ball, shot straight into him.

Need. She was wild with need.

And he couldn't seem to get enough of it. Of her.

The part of him that trusted no one, and her least of all, didn't trust this reaction either.

But the rest of him—especially the hardest part of him—didn't care.

Because she tasted like magic and he had given up on magic long, long time ago.

Because her hands tangled in his hair and tugged his face to hers, and he didn't have it in him to question that.

All Atlas knew was that he wanted more. Needed more.

As if, after surviving things that no man should be forced to bear, it would be little Lexi Haring who took him out. It would be this one shockingly pretty woman who would be the end of him. And not because she'd plotted against him, as he believed some if not all of her family had done, but because of this. Her surrender.

The endless, wondrous glory of her surrender.

Continue reading
IMPRISONED BY THE
GREEK'S RING
Caitlin Crews

Available next month
www.millsandboon.co.uk

LET'S TALK

Romance

For exclusive extracts, competitions
and special offers, find us online:

f facebook.com/millsandboon

⬛ @millsandboonuk

🐦 @millsandboon

Or get in touch on 0844 844 1351*

For all the latest titles coming soon, visit
millsandboon.co.uk/nextmonth